The Ghost Files

Volume 4 - Part 1

By Apryl Baker

The Ghost Files Volume 4 – Part 1

Copyright © 2016 by Apryl Baker.
All rights reserved.
Second Print Edition: August 2018

Limitless Publishing, LLC
Kailua, HI 96734
www.limitlesspublishing.com

Formatting: Limitless Publishing

ISBN-13: 978-1-64034-994-0

Dedication

For all the foster kids out there who
believe they don't have a voice.
You do.
All you have to do is speak up.

Chapter One

Liar.

That one word screams over and over into my head as I stare at the picture of me and my mom. Doc is babbling, but I haven't heard a word of it. All I can focus on is that he *lied* to me. He knew who I was when he got my email all those months ago. I trusted him, told him *everything*!

The only people who have never lied to me are a demon who's decided I'm his new pet project, and my father, who's a bad man himself. He admits it, doesn't apologize for it, but he doesn't lie. I snort at the stupidity of it. The only people I can trust are the very ones I shouldn't.

"Mattie, *please* listen to me."

Because your mother gave it to me…

Lawrence Olivet, spook doctor extraordinaire, and my friend.

Or so I thought.

He knew my mom, knew me. Why would she give him a picture of us? Did she tell him what I could do? Is that why he was so eager to get to know me, worked so hard to make me trust him? What's his angle?

"I'm not the enemy, Mattie," Doc says softly. "I just want to help you."

"By lying to me?" I shout the words, but I try to stay calm. "How did you get in the house?"

He runs a hand through his dark brown hair. "There was a key under the doormat. Not a very good hiding spot."

No, it isn't, but that I can fix.

Doc takes a step toward me and I automatically take one back. The sink is right behind me, and Mrs. Cross keeps her knives in their block right beside the dish drainer. My hand inches toward it. I have a weapon if I need it.

"Do you honestly think I would hurt you?" There is no mistaking the wounded sound in his voice.

"I don't know." I remember the crazy look in his eyes when I first got here. He'd reminded me of Silas, the demon who knows way too much about me. Silas scares the bejesus out of me.

He makes a sound like a growl and the demonic look creeps back in his eyes, and I shiver. It's hard to describe. His eyes remind me of a frozen lake you are walking on, and then just when you think you're safe, it cracks and you go under.

"Mattie, all I've ever wanted is to make sure you're safe. I had planned to tell you everything that first day. It was my intention from the moment you contacted me. Then I met you, and realized you wouldn't be as receptive as I'd hoped. You have serious trust issues and I *needed* you to trust me. When you told me about your father, I knew I had to tell you the truth. You needed to know why your mother was scared enough to send you away with Amanda. All I want is to protect you, Mattie. I swear to all that's holy, it's the only intention I've ever had."

My head is pounding and I can't think. After Meg and Jake dying right in front of me tonight, this is all too much. I need to scream, to cry, to hit something…or someone. All the emotions I've been barely holding at bay start to build up—the anger, the fury, and the pain.

Doc's eyes go wide and he takes several steps away from me. I'm guessing my own eyes have gone black. They seem to be doing that a lot since Dan almost died. Something snapped in me during those three days I sat by his hospital bed, begging him not to leave me. I can't seem to stomp down my need to cause others pain anymore. Right now, that need is directed at Doc.

"Mattie, you need to calm down." He slides farther away from me. "I'm not going to hurt you. If you'll just let me explain…"

"No, I don't need to calm down. You *lied* to me, and I don't trust you anymore. What I'm going to do is walk out the door, and I want you gone before Mary and her mom get back." My voice is low and calm, but there's a definite bite to it.

"Do you understand?"

He nods, but I don't think he understands, not really. "I'm staying at The Hilton, room three-oh-four," he says. "When you calm down and want to talk, just call or stop by. I'm here when you're ready."

I snort. Not a chance of that happening anytime soon. If I can get out of here without him hurting me or me hurting him, I'll count it as a blessing. There's just something about the look in his eyes that puts my senses on red alert. I square my shoulders and stride purposefully toward the doorway, keeping my eyes on Doc the entire time. Once I hit the living room, I grab my bag off the chair and am out the door, pulling it closed behind me.

Dan meets me halfway, a frown on his face. I shake my head and push him back toward the car. I don't want him anywhere near Doc, not yet. I have to figure all this out first.

"What's wrong?" he asks, confused. "Your eyes…they're black."

I close them and take several deep breaths, concentrating on Dan and how happy I am that he's alive. Dan always centers me. I open my eyes. "Better?"

"Yeah, but what…"

"I'll explain later." I don't want to get into it right now. "Promise."

I groan when my father, Ezekiel Crane, gets out of the car, concerned. Great. I so do not need Zeke and Doc meeting just yet.

"Just a ghost." A ghost from my past I never even knew was there. "After everything that's happened tonight, I can't deal with it."

"Of course not." Zeke steps out of the way so Dan and I can get in. "I had to remove the ghost-proofing from the apartment because of your…er…"

"Danny Phantom syndrome?" I supply with a weak smile. Seems I have collected so much ghost energy, the things that ward ghosts away also keep me from entering as well.

Zeke cocks his head and stares at me, his expression full of questions.

"It's a cartoon about a boy who had so much ghost energy, he could turn into a ghost when he wanted to."

"You have this ability, *ma petite*?" Zeke's eyes are wide with shock.

"No." I snuggle into Dan, careful to keep my sprained wrist out of the way. "I was just using it as an analogy."

Zeke's eyes narrow, but he doesn't say anything about me wrapped around Dan. Dan has been through a lot tonight. He lost Meg. She died because my ex-boyfriend's brother was obsessed with her and decided to exercise his serial killer tendencies. Everything bad that's happened to Dan always seems to center around me. He says he doesn't blame me, but this time is different. Meg *died*. Once the shock wears off, I have to wonder if he'll come to hate me. Even now, I think he's already distancing himself. He's limp, not pushing me away, but not pulling me closer either, and it worries me.

"I have a few experts working on ways to adapt the ghost-proofing to your unique situation," Zeke continues. "This has never happened before, at least not that I can find. We may need some of the experts to test you…"

"Test me?" I sit up, instantly suspicious after the confrontation with Doc. "Test me for what, exactly?"

"How your energy interacts with the barriers set up to keep ghosts out," Zeke explains patiently. "If we don't know the how and the why, we can't find a good fix for it. We need to be able to keep the ghosts out so I can keep you safe."

Zeke's blue eyes are open and honest, and I believe him. He only wants to help me. Usually his eyes are full of secrets. Once again, I'm struck by how much he looks like the actor who plays Ichabod Crane on Fox's *Sleepy Hollow*. I think it's the shoulder length hair and the nose. He just looks like the guy.

Nodding, I sit back, noticing Dan hasn't moved. I'm worried about him. Maybe he's in shock. He's way too pale. The man shouldn't even be out of the hospital after the brain injury he suffered a few days ago. Which was my fault too. Silas used Dan as a guinea pig for a demonic rune he wanted to use on me. If Dan survived, so would I.

Dan nearly died, was supposed to die,

but I fought with another Reaper to keep him with me. I understood the consequences, knew it would cost people their lives. But at the time, I didn't care. All that mattered was keeping Dan alive. It ended up costing him Meg. If Dan *had* died, she'd have been home grieving instead of at the stupid party where we both got nabbed. She'd be alive…but Dan would be dead, and there's not a scenario where I could ever live with that.

"I have a doctor meeting us at the penthouse." Zeke interrupts my thoughts. "I think the boy's in shock."

"I think you're right," I agree. Dan doesn't even blink. I'm not sure he even heard us. "Maybe we should just take him back to the hospital."

"It will be fine, *ma petite*. I will let nothing happen to your friend. I promise. If the doctor recommends taking him to the hospital, then that's what we'll do."

"I can't lose him." Not after everyone else I've lost. I can't lose Dan.

"You won't." Zeke's voice is confident. "I swear it."

I want to believe him, but no one can promise that, not even Dan.

"Did you collect any clothes, Mattie?"

I shake my head, glancing down at my bag. It only had my wallet, my sketchpad, and some charcoal pencils. "Ghost, remember?"

Zeke pulls out his phone and starts texting. Lord only knows what he's up to. If he can produce a toothbrush, I really don't care. It's been a long night.

When we pull into the private parking garage of Zeke's high rise, I'm relieved. It only takes a few minutes to ride up to the top floor, but Dan's just going through the motions. He's freaking me out, so much that I'm able to forget about Doc for a few minutes. This is not good. Maybe we should take him back to the hospital. Zeke's butler, Montgomery, opens the door, grim-faced, and ushers us into the massive living room. The promised doctor rises from the chair he'd been sitting in, takes one look at Dan, and has Montgomery help him take Dan down the hall. To one of the guest bedrooms, I'm guessing.

"He'll be fine, Mattie," Zeke says. "Mrs. Banks went shopping and picked a few things up for you and Daniel while we were on our way over. The only place open this early is that Walmart store. I hope everything will be to your satisfaction."

"Walmart's fine. I shop there all the time." A small smile almost manages to break free at the grimace on Zeke's face. I doubt he's ever even been inside a Walmart. I'm going to have to introduce him to the finer things available at 4:00 a.m. that can only be found in Wally World, as I affectionately call Walmart.

"Are you okay?" he asks softly, coming to stand in front of me. "Everyone's been focused on Daniel because of Megan's death, but I haven't forgotten the fact you almost died yourself tonight. If you hadn't been able to fight, neither of you would have stood a chance. You'd be dead yourself, Emma Rose." The name he'd given me at birth slips out, unbidden. His hand trembles as he places it on my shoulder. I can feel his hesitation. He's not sure how I'll

11

respond. "I owe Daniel and the Malone boys a great debt. I owe them your life."

I do something I've wanted to do since I first met Zeke. I wrap my arms around him and bury my face in his shirt. He stills, shocked, but then pulls me into the same kind of bear hug Dan usually does after a near death experience. He and I were only reunited a few weeks ago, haven't really gotten the chance to spend any time together, but at the same time, we have a connection I can't define. He's my dad. Maybe it's as simple as that.

"Shhh, *ma petite*," he whispers. "You're safe now."

For the first time in almost a year, I believe those words. I've never had a dad before, but I always imagined what it would be like to have one. Zeke may not be the best dad in the world, but he's mine. And he makes me feel safe.

I pull back and offer him a small smile. "I'm going to get cleaned up and then check on Dan. Where can I take a shower?"

"Your bathroom, if you'd like. It has that soaker tub…" I'm shaking my head even before he finishes. I just managed to escape several angry ghost girls who had been trying to drown me for a week and almost accomplished it. Eli had to give me CPR to bring me back. Nope, no more tubs for me for a good long while. Zeke understands almost immediately. He'd come to see me in the hospital after the drowning. "Your bathroom has a shower in it as well."

I give Zeke another brief hug and then grab my bag and the Walmart bags sitting by the stairwell before heading up to find my room. I do remember where it is. On the way, I pass the guest rooms, but the doors are closed, so I limp down the hall to my own. It's still barren. Zeke and I haven't had the chance to go furniture shopping, but my bathroom? Now, that's decked out as only a bathroom should be with a massive antique soaker tub, shower that has three shower heads, and is bigger than my and Mary's room put together at the Cross house. I love it.

I turn on the shower to let the tiles heat up. I hate stepping into a cold shower. My reflection in the mirror catches my attention, and I grimace at what I see staring back. I'm a mess. My face is bruised and I have a cut that's stitched above my eye, which is already purpling up. My hair is matted with blood, and my left arm is encased in a brace. While I hadn't broken my arm, I'd done some damage that requires seeing an orthopedic surgeon tomorrow. I could almost laugh if I wasn't in so much pain. I look like I've survived the zombie apocalypse.

Gingerly, I remove the brace, not wanting to get it wet, and then strip out of the dress in record time. It's covered in Meg's blood. I have no desire to ever see it again. I ball it up and stuff it in the trash can, hoping the housekeeping staff will take the hint. My shoulder gives me a bit of a fit. The bullet had only grazed my arm, but I'd wrenched the whole shoulder somehow. I'm still not sure how I managed that one. I wasn't even aware of how much it hurt until the hospital x-rayed it. They'd started twisting and turning it, and I'd started snarling. I think they like to torture me when it comes to x-rays.

My poor body is covered in bruises, scrapes, and small cuts. When the hot water hits all the fresh wounds, I hiss at the sting of pain. I watch the stream of red water as it runs over me and pools around the drain. Blood. Meg's blood, my blood.

She's dead. She's really dead. I bite back a sob. I've been mad at her for weeks, and she was trying *so* hard to make it right, to be my friend again. I was such a witch to her, and now I can't make it right. I sit down and just let the hot water wash over me. I don't have the strength to stand. She's gone. My best friend is gone, and I can't bring her back. I try to keep my sobbing quiet as I rock back and forth in the shower, letting the hot water wash away Meg's blood and my tears.

I can't let Dan see me like this. He needs me to be strong. He's been there for me through everything, and now it's my turn to do the same thing for him. I have to get it together. Pushing up, I grab up the shower gel and scrub the rest of the blood from my battered body. My hair is a little harder because of my arm and my shoulder. I have to sit down to accomplish that one. At least Zeke stocked my favorite scent—strawberries. The soap and the shampoo both smell like strawberries.

Once I'm as clean as I can get without causing myself any more damage, I towel off as best I can and dig out a pair of clean underwear as well as flannel PJs. Mrs. Banks is a saint. She'd gotten me the warmest material around. Not only that, but there is toothpaste, a toothbrush, and deodorant. After taking care of my sewer mouth, I put my brace back on and grab my bag before padding back out into the hallway.

The door to one of the guest rooms is cracked. I hurry down and peek in. Dan's sound asleep. He's clean too. The doctor must have had him take a hot shower to try to warm him up. People in shock need to stay warm. The curtains are open and the soft light from the moon hits his face. He looks vulnerable and lost, even asleep. How am I going to get him through this?

I go plop down in the chair over by the window and turn on the table lamp. My first instinct is to crawl into bed with him, but he needs warmth, and my body temperature always runs cold thanks to the ghost energy I've collected. I might make him worse if I cuddle up next to him. So, I'll draw. It's the one thing that might settle me down.

My bag feels heavier than usual. Frowning, I open it and see the photo album Zeke gave me the other day. I'd forgotten about it. There are pictures of my family in there. I pull it out and stare at the cover. My family. Proof I had people who'd loved me. Proof of a father, a mother, and grandparents. It's all right here. I just have to open it and look.

My hand shakes a little bit as I hold the album. I'd shoved it in my bag so I could think about it later. I put everything off until later that might cause me some pain. It's a habit of mine. If Dan had known about the album, he'd have made me look through it the same day Zeke gave it to me.

I lay the album on my lap and open it. The first picture I see floors me.

It's a photo of my father and my birth mother, laughing and looking happy.

The problem? I've seen her before.

Chapter Two

I'd had a vision of a woman sitting in a field with her little boy and her baby. I'd thought they were ghosts at first, that the woman didn't know they were dead. She'd been so upset when I asked her about the children's father. Was the little girl me? Had I seen myself when I was just a baby? That woman was my mother?

So many questions rattle around in my head. What had I actually seen? Was it a vision or, maybe I'd seen inside my mother's mind? Zeke said she was in a catatonic state and no one had been able to reach her because she blamed herself for my kidnapping.

Or so we'd all thought. According to

Doc, my mother had sent me away with the woman who'd raised me. My head hurt trying to sort out all the secrets. Maybe Claire had told Doc that my mother sent me away, and that was the only truth he knew. Seriously, who in their right mind would admit to kidnapping?

One thing doesn't make sense. If my mother sent me away, why would she have collapsed into a catatonic state? Zeke said her guilt drove her nuts, but why feel guilty if she was trying to protect me?

I need to go see Melissa. Since I can talk to her in my dreams, maybe she'll hear my voice and realize I'm not gone anymore, that I'm home. Or maybe she is so far gone, no one can reach her. Either way, I want to try. She's my family, and I'd grown up in the foster care system with no one. I am not about to simply forget her because she's got some mental issues.

Dan is still passed out, so I close the album and go back downstairs to find Zeke. He's in his office, cell phone in hand, pacing. He sounds frustrated and more than a little irritated. There's a cold bite to his voice that sends shivers down my spine. He never uses this tone around me, and I can see the man everyone tried to warn me about, the ruthless man who has done very bad things.

"I told you, Mama, she's not ready to see anyone yet." He pauses while he listens. "She's *my* daughter, and my answer is *no*."

Even I can hear the woman screech from over here. "Ezekiel David Crane, don't you dare speak to me like that!"

Zeke's eyes close briefly and he takes a deep breath. "I'm sorry, Mama." He listens, and before he can say anything else, his mother hangs up on him. At least that's what I think she did, because he stares at it nonplussed.

It's funny to see Zeke flustered. He's usually so self-assured and more than a little scary. It humanizes him.

He turns and sees me in the doorway and his expression becomes alarmed. "Is everything all right, *ma petite*?"

"Yeah, sorry. I didn't want to

interrupt."

His aggravation comes back. "No, it is I that am sorry. My parents will not be put off anymore, especially after tonight's events. They are catching the first flight out of New Orleans. I have tried to keep them from bombarding you until you get more comfortable with the situation."

"It's okay." Inside I'm freaking out at the thought of my grandparents coming to meet me, but I push it down. I have more important things to deal with at the moment.

"You don't know my parents." He runs a hand over his face, much like I tend to do when I'm frustrated. It makes me smile a little to see something we share. "I guess we shall worry about them when they arrive. Now, *ma petite*, did you need something?"

I hold up the photo album. "Do you have a minute to answer some questions?"

The smile that spreads across his face tugs at my heart. I'm struck again that I have a father who loves me. It still boggles my mind.

"Come sit." He gestures toward the couch sitting against one wall and I follow him over. It's as soft as it looks.

I open the album to the first page. "This is my mother?"

"Yes, that is Melissa," he confirms.

"I've seen her before," I blurt out.

"What?" He gives me the same nonplussed look he'd had a moment before. "That's impossible, Mattie. Your mother has been in a comatose state for the last thirteen years."

"It was a dream…well…vision might be a better word."

Zeke cocks his head, but waits for me to continue.

"I dreamt of this woman sitting in a field with her two kids. One was a baby, and the little boy was about five or six, I think. I thought they were all ghosts and she didn't know it, but when I saw this picture…"

"There was a little boy there?" Zeke asks, a frown marring his face.

I nod, deciding to trust my father with Silas's bombshell. "Silas said I had a brother."

"What?" he nearly shouts.

"He said you didn't know about him because he wasn't yours."

"That demon lies quite frequently." Zeke stands and goes to pour himself a drink from the small bar he has in the office.

"Not this time," I say. "Silas has never lied to me, and besides, in my dream, there *was* a little boy."

Zeke mutters something I can't hear and starts to pace. "How often does the demon speak with you?"

"He pops up randomly. Caleb demon-proofed the house for me so he can't just show up in my bedroom anymore."

The look Zeke gives me is one of fury, but it's not directed at me. He's not happy about Silas showing up in my bedroom. I had been none-to-pleased at the time either.

"I don't know that much about Melissa's family," Zeke admits. "She was very closemouthed about them, as I told you before. After we admitted her into the hospital, I tried to find them, but

I discovered a few things about your mother."

My eyes widen. He said it so ominously.

"When I met Melissa, I was enamored. She was beautiful and very mysterious. The more time I spent with her, the fonder I grew of her. When she discovered she was pregnant, I offered to marry her, but she refused. This much I have told you."

He takes a long drink of the amber liquid in his tumbler and settles himself on the edge of his desk.

"She would never talk about her family. It upset her to think of them, but I don't know why. I had assumed they were estranged, or possibly that she had no living relatives. I didn't know. She wouldn't speak of them at all. In truth, it didn't really concern me. We were happy at that point."

"I hear a but?" I sit back and pull my legs up, tucking my feet under me Indian style on the comfy sofa.

"But she started to change once you were born." He downs the rest of his drink, and I can't help but to think he seems to be trying to fortify himself.

"Your mother adored you," he told me. "She used to sit and watch you sleep for hours when you were born. As you grew, she started to look at you differently. I never doubted that she loved you, *ma petite*, but I became concerned for your safety."

"My safety?"

"You asked me when we first met if I would ever sacrifice you to gain more power. I wouldn't, but I don't know if the same could be said of Melissa. I walked in on her one day, her hand over your face. It scared me. I hired a nanny the next day."

My eyes widen. My birth mother tried to kill me too?

"She said she was simply trying to put you to sleep, rubbing her hand up and down your face. I'd seen her do it often enough. You had to be coaxed to sleep when you were a baby." A smile ghosts across his face at the memory.

"You didn't believe her?"

He sighs deeply. "I still don't know the

answer to that question. She watched you a lot, and her look was more calculating than anything else. I don't tell you this to try and sway your opinion on your mother. I'm only trying to explain some things you need to know."

I really don't want to believe that both my mothers tried to kill me, but from what Zeke is saying, it appears they did. Aren't I the lucky one?

"I had a bad feeling the day I left for a business meeting in Dallas. I knew I shouldn't have gone, but I trusted Amanda to watch over you. She adored you and gave you the love your mother seemed to be unable to give you during those last weeks you were with us. She'd become withdrawn, depressed. I was worried and had already spoken with her about seeing someone for her depression. When I came home to discover her locked in her room and you missing..." He closes his eyes and a look of pain crosses his face.

"Locked in her room?" I ask, confused. Why would she be locked in her room?

"I told you she became worse in the

final weeks before your kidnapping. I started finding her in your room at all hours of the night, staring at you oddly. It scared the devil out of me. So much so that I moved Amanda's bed into your nursery. I put a lock on the outside of our door for those nights I had to be away. I didn't trust her not to hurt you or Amanda. I was so concerned about what your mother might do to you that I failed to notice the attachment Amanda had formed."

He blames himself for my kidnapping. "It wasn't your fault."

"Whose fault it was or was not is moot now." He smiles sadly. "I'm just sorry you grew up the way you did."

"Don't be," I tell him. "I'm not. My mom might not have been a perfect mother, and yes, she was a junkie, but she loved me. Even now, knowing what I do, I can still say that because I think in her own way, she was trying to protect me. In her mind, killing me saved me. I would be safe from everyone and everything. I know it's hard for you to hear, but Claire, or Amanda as you know her, *was* my mom, and I love my mama." That is a truth I finally accepted, and I am okay with it now.

Zeke stands and comes over to sit beside me. "It *is* hard for me, *ma petite*. She took you away from me, and I don't know if I can ever forgive her for that. I do understand, though, that you loved her and that she was your mother. No one could ever tell me my mother didn't love me, because like you, I love my mama. I won't ever try to take that away from you. I'm trying to understand that she took you to protect you from Melissa, but it's difficult. I need time, *ma petite*, to wrap my head around it and start to forgive her."

Telling him Claire took me to keep me safe from him is not something I'm gonna say. Let him believe what he wants. Unless Melissa wakes up and says otherwise, he'll never know, and telling him would hurt him. It's not something I'm prepared to do.

"We're off topic." Zeke straightens and leans back against the couch. "When your mother slipped into her comatose state, I tried to find her family. I hired the best private investigators money could buy, and they all came up empty. Melissa was very good at covering her tracks. I don't even think her name was Melissa Roux."

A thought struck me and I gasped. "Wait. In the dream, she said her name was Georgina...Georgina Dubois, and her son's name was Jacob."

Zeke nods, his face troubled. "You're sure she said Dubois?"

"Yeah, is that a bad thing?"

"Maybe. I have to do some digging first."

This doesn't bode well at all. He looks more than worried. He looks a little scared. "Why is her last name a bad thing?"

His eyes are troubled when he finally speaks. "The Dubois family, at least the one that runs in our supernatural circles, is deeply rooted in the black arts. Our family may deal with demons when we need to, but their family relies on demons for many things. The deals they've made..." He shakes his head in disgust. "You mother, however, may not be involved in that particular family. There are many Dubois in Louisiana. Let's not borrow trouble unless we have to, okay?"

I think my face has grown paler because his eyes widen with worry. My mother's family dealt in demons too? Silas keeps telling me I belong to him. What if I do? What if Melissa or someone in her family promised me to Silas? Did they make a deal with me as the demon's price? My hands start to shake, and Zeke's worry grows to full-out alarm.

"*Ma petite*, what's wrong?"

"Do you think…maybe, the reason Silas keeps popping up is because of some kind of deal Melissa made with him?"

"I don't know." True worry colors his tone. "But be assured, if that is the case, the demon owes me enough favors, it won't make a difference if she did do something like that. You are my child, and no one, living, dead, or supernatural will ever harm you."

I look up and get a good look at the very bad man who is my father. His face is fierce, hard, and cold all at once. He means every word, and it scares me. I don't want him to hurt anyone in his attempt to protect me. I have this feeling that no matter what he does, he can't protect me from what Silas has planned. I don't know what Silas wants, but I think it's major. He wouldn't have gone through so much trouble keeping me alive otherwise.

"Can I ask you a question, Zeke?"

"Of course." He's starting to calm down a little.

"My grandparents...did they know what the oracle told you about me?"

"You don't pull any punches, do you?" he asks ruefully. "Yes, your grandparents know what the oracle said. They never believed I'd be able to murder my own child to gain her powers."

"Why not?"

"Because of how much they love me. My mother said once I held you, I'd understand her faith in me because I would love you as much as she does me. And I do."

"So I don't have to worry about them

plotting to kill me, then?" I try to make it a joke, but I am quite serious. It seems everyone in my family has, at one point or another, wanted to see me dead. It's unnerving.

That causes Zeke to laugh. "I'd like to see someone try to hurt you around my mother. I was with her when I got the call they may have found you. It's the first time I've seen my mother cry since my sister died when I was just a boy. Trust me, sweetheart, your grandmother will protect you with her dying breath."

Relief swamps me. One less thing to worry about.

"I'm gonna head back upstairs." I stand. "I need to make sure Dan's okay."

"Of course," Zeke murmurs. "I'll make a few calls and see if we can find this missing brother of yours."

I start to walk away, but stop. "Zeke?"

"Hmm?" he asks, not really paying attention. I can tell his focus has shifted to Melissa and the information I've given him.

"I just wanted to say thank you for everything."

"You don't need to thank me, Mattie. I'm your father, and I'm supposed to take care of you."

"I know, but it's been a long time since anyone has cared this much about me. I haven't had anyone do that since my mom died, so thank you."

I turn and rush out of the room before he can say anything.

Talking about my feelings is something I hate doing. It upsets me because showing any kind of emotion growing up in foster care made you weak and a target to be bullied. I know that's the wrong stance to take, but it's what I know, and breaking old habits is harder than one would think.

I have a family who really loves me, and I'm terrified. What if I mess up? What if I disappoint them? I didn't grow up with money, and they come from old money. Zeke oozes proper manners, and his speech is so cultured. It makes me feel inferior. No matter what he says, I know appearances are important to him, and most likely my grandparents too.

The cold slaps me in the face at the top

of the stairs. I'd been so involved in stressing out over meeting my grandparents and everything Zeke told me about my mother, I didn't pay attention as I ran up the stairs.

I'm paying attention now.

The hallway is dark, the only light coming from a cracked door at the end of the hall. There's something here, even if I don't see it. Zeke had to take down the ghost-proofing so I could enter the house. Anything could be in here. Where is it?

I take two steps forward and wince as a blast of cold hits me. It seeps into my bones, a slow, icy burn. Emotions flood me, and I almost fall under the weight of them. It's unlike anything I've ever felt, and I've come up against some pretty scary stuff. This thing is hurt and angry and full of rage.

"Hello?" I whisper.

The bathroom door swings open, and I glance that way, unwilling to move closer. I can hear the dripping of the water.

The cold intensifies, and a sheen of frost starts to cover the walls.

Ice forms at the base of the bathroom door, and I watch as it starts to spread out, like a spider's web, and creeps toward me, speeding faster and faster down the hallway.

The air becomes icy cold and dry. It burns my throat as I breathe in, watching the ice crawl down the hall.

Well, fudgepops. This isn't good at all.

The door to my left creaks, and I freeze.

Don't look, don't look, don't look.

I close my eyes and refuse to look.

Someone whispers in my ear, and the pain that explodes in my head rips a scream out of me. I fall to my knees and place both hands over my ears. The cold bites into me, and I know it's touching me. I can feel it.

I open my eyes and look up, and I can't help it.

I scream.

Chapter Three

Dan

A sigh of relief escapes when she leaves my room. Pretending to sleep is harder than it sounds. I know she just wants to help me, but right now, I can't deal with her.

The guilt is eating me alive. My girlfriend is lying dead in the morgue, and the only thing going through my head is thank God it's not Mattie. How messed up is that? When I saw Meg go down, I didn't even look at her. Panic hit me, and the only person I looked for was my Squirt. My one and only thought was to make sure Mattie was safe. Meg was my girlfriend. I should have thought of her first.

But I didn't.

Mattie Louise Hathaway. The girl turned my world upside down in more ways than one. I want to hate her, to be able to walk away and not look back. I want my old life back, my family intact. I just want everything to go back to the way it was. I wish I could walk away from her, but I can't. God knows I've tried, but something keeps drawing me back to her. Some force of nature won't let me say goodbye.

I sigh and roll over, feeling a little numb. I'm not the same person I was a year ago. I don't know if that's a good thing or not. Sometimes I think it is because I grew up a lot. I've made some hard choices over the last few months as well. As hard as my life is, I can't say I'd change it. Even though my mom ended up in jail, I found my biological family. I can't regret that. My dad taught my brother and me that family is everything, so I can't regret the Malones, even if it means my mother being arrested for kidnapping and murder.

I agreed to help Mattie find her father, and in doing so, I uncovered the truth about my own mother. Ann Richards had kidnapped my birth mother and killed her after I was born. She staged an accident with the help of her sister, who we found out kidnapped Mattie from her parents. Ann raised me and loved me. I don't doubt that. She's my mom. If the Malones can't deal with that, so be it. I'm not turning my back on her.

That's just one instance of Mattie causing my life to be turned upside down. She doesn't mean to. All she wanted was to find her family. It's not her fault my mother did what she did. Secrets have a way of coming out, and if not Mattie, eventually the truth would have come out another way.

Mattie blames herself for everything bad that's happened to me, but she shouldn't. None of it was her fault. Not really. *I* don't blame her. I wish she would see herself like I do. She's this beautiful, loving person who is loyal to a fault. She's also the strongest person I've ever met. Growing up in foster care, surviving being kidnapped and tortured, and then surviving a psychopath who was obsessed with her—she's tough as nails. I don't know if I could have come out the other side stronger for it.

I went from a guy who only believed in what he could see, what he could touch, to a guy who can't deny the existence of the supernatural. I've seen ghosts, demons, and even an angel. I also discovered how selfish I am.

It's my fault Meg is dead. When I was dying, the reaper warned me coming back meant innocent people would die. It was my time to go, and staying would disrupt the balance of life and death. Leaving meant abandoning Mattie, never seeing her smile again or hearing that horrible laugh of hers. I couldn't do it. She meant more to me than anyone or anything. Still does. If I had died, though, Meg would be alive. Her death is on me. It was my choice to be selfish.

What really bothers me is if the choice had been about Meg and not Mattie, I may have gone on. If I'd never met my Squirt, I would have done the right thing and died. I wouldn't have stayed for Meg.

The pain of losing Meg is there. It cuts deep, makes my entire body ache, but relief that Mattie is safe outweighs even my grief.

So what does that say about me?

I can admit, at least to myself, that I have feelings for Mattie. Feelings that go beyond friendship or family. Because of her age, I ignored them. I don't know what to do about them, though. I don't really even understand them. I only know that I need to keep her safe and happy, that simply being near her makes me happy. Caleb told me our blood is designed to keep Mattie safe, to want her happy. We were made to protect people like her, that it's hardwired into our DNA. Maybe it's as simple as that.

God, I hope it's as simple as that.

A scream breaks the silence of the night. I'm up and running, tearing the door open. The first thing I notice is how dark the hallway is. None of the lights are on, and I shiver, feeling the cold creep up along my spine. I've never felt anything like this before. It seeps into my bones, chilling them. When I let out the breath I've been holding, fog appears in front of me. The darkness creeps closer, wrapping around me. Fear splinters through my mind, but I force it back. Mattie needs me.

My gaze sweeps the hallway, looking for her. I hear a whimper and look down. She's on her knees on the floor, hands covering her ears.

"Mattie?" I whisper, searching the dark hall. I don't see anything, but it's so cold. Freezing. I take a step forward and flinch at the frigid air that hits me in the face.

"Don't." The word is whispered, but I hear it. She's looking not at me, but at something in front of her. All I see is empty space.

"What is it?"

"Mattie!"

Zeke runs up the stairs and he stops, his eyes wide. "Dear God."

"What?" I demand, unable to see what they see. I step forward and put my hand on her shoulder, intending to haul her up, but I fall to my knees, my hand gripping her shoulder so hard, it's going to leave a bruise.

The thing in front of us is horrific. Bent and bloody, the stringy brown hair is matted with blood. It might have been a little girl at some point, but what is holding onto Mattie is no longer a little girl. It's full of pain and rage. Black eyes settle on me, and I cringe. The stench is terrible. Her hands are purple, two fingers missing. Yellow pus drips from her nostrils and onto the floor between her and Mattie. Her white t-shirt with little purple flowers on it is covered in black stains. What in God's name happened to her?

It screams something, and Mattie cries out in pain. Whatever it's doing, it's hurting her. "How do I help her?"

"Help me pull her away from it." Zeke is on her other side, and I stand, keeping one hand on her shoulder so I can see the thing. We jerk her up and back, breaking the hold the thing has on her. It screams wordlessly, and Zeke reaches into his pocket, throwing something at it. Whatever it was it works. The little nasty disappears. Salt, maybe?

"Mattie?" Zeke's worried expression mirrors my own. Her eyes are glazed and she's shaking.

"We need to get her warm." I swing her up in my arms, following Zeke downstairs to his study. A fire blazes in the hearth, and I head straight for it. Her father gives me a throw from the couch, and I wrap her in it as best I can. "Why isn't she saying anything?"

"I don't know. Let me call a friend. He may know how to help her."

Mattie makes a strangled sound, and I pull her closer. She's shaking, but I don't think it's from cold. Shock, maybe? Zeke is on the phone, but he's pouring salt across windowsills and the doorway as he talks. I dig my own phone out and call Dr. Olivet. If anyone knows how to help, he might.

"Dan?" The relief in the doctor's voice is palpable. "Is she okay?"

"Well, no, that's why I'm calling." I quickly explain the situation, but I have a niggling feeling in the back of my mind all isn't right. Something is going on with the doc.

"It sounds like shock," Dr. Olivet says. "I'm not surprised, given everything she's been through. Get her to the hospital if she's not any better in about thirty minutes. Where are you, by the way?"

"We're at her father's."

"What?" Dr. Olivet explodes, and I pull the phone away from my ear. "Why are you there? Don't you know how dangerous he is?"

"Mattie wanted to come here, so we're here." What is going on? He's gone from calm to super excited in less than two seconds. "I'm with her, Doctor. She's safe with me."

He lets out a strangled sigh. "Dan, just don't leave her alone with him. No matter what happens, don't leave her alone. Ever. Promise me."

"I promise, Dr. Olivet." I need to do some more investigating on Zeke if the doc is this upset. "I'll call you if she gets worse."

"Please do, Dan. If you need anything, call me. Doesn't matter what time."

"I will," I murmur and disconnect the call. Something is going on there. Maybe when Mattie wakes up she can tell me more.

Mattie's fingers claw into my side, and I rub her back, trying to comfort her, while I attempt to remember how to treat shock. "Dr. Olivet says it sounds like shock. Can the doctor who was here before come back?"

"Yes." Zeke lays a hand on her head. "She's so cold."

"Mattie's always cold." I should call Eli, but the thought of it has me pulling her closer. I don't want my brother near her, even if he can warm her up. Never did. I only did what I had to in order to keep the peace. "Bring me two of those throw pillows. We need to get her feet up." Zeke hurries to do as I ask. There is real worry in his eyes. I think Doc is wrong about him, at least in regard to Mattie.

He sits beside us and arranges her feet. "The physician is on his way back." He pulls her shoes off and starts to rub her feet. "Did you see what attacked her?"

"Not until I touched her."

"You saw it only after you touched her?" He looks up sharply. "Has that ever happened before?"

"No," I say slowly. "Why?"

"Daniel, your people see only the souls that have gone dark. What was here was a child, a very terrified child. Its soul was on the verge of turning from all the torment it has gone through. Someone mutilated that child, put it through horrors that defy reality. I thought maybe you had seen it in the moment its soul went dark."

"Maybe." I don't think so, though.

"It was trying to tell us something, but it didn't know how to communicate." He pauses, thinking. "Have you been watching the news at all?"

"I haven't turned on a television in days." I'd been in the hospital, unconscious.

"Are you aware of the children who have been murdered in the city over the last month or so?"

My mouth falls open into a silent "oh." Was that thing one of the children who had gone missing, only to turn up dead? Had it searched out Mattie to try to tell her what happened to it? "Yeah," I say after a minute. "It's an ongoing investigation at the precinct."

"I have a feeling my daughter is going to get dragged into that mess." Zeke lets out a frustrated sigh. "She isn't ready for any of this. She doesn't know how to defend herself against their attacks, how to sort out the information, how to help them without hurting herself. I need to train her, but I don't think we are going to have time. This situation is more than it seems."

"What do you mean?"

"Have you ever heard the name Deleriel?"

"No."

"He's a fallen angel, one of the first demons. His specialty was feeding off the tormented souls of children. He hasn't roamed this Earth for centuries, but he does come up to feed every so often. I think that is who we are dealing with."

"What makes you think it's a demon instead of a sick pedophile?"

Zeke let out a harsh laugh. "The stench coming from the child. It smelled of sulphur. Only a demon or a victim of a demon smells of that. We may need help."

"Help?"

"You fight a demon with a demon." Zeke stands and faces the room, his back to us. "*Silas*!"

What the…he's calling Silas here?

Minutes go by and I can see Zeke's anger spiking. The demon is ignoring him. "Silas!"

"Maybe he's busy?" I suggest. I do not want Silas anywhere near Mattie, not to mention I might not be able to keep from attacking him myself after what he'd done to me. It was his fault I almost died.

Zeke starts to pace, muttering. "He never fails to come when I summon him."

The butler interrupts whatever he was going to say by announcing the arrival of the doctor. He has me bring Squirt to the couch where he can examine her. Zeke and I stand impatiently and wait. She's so cold. If she doesn't warm up soon, I'll call Eli, despite my feelings about it. She's more important to me than my own petty jealousy.

"It's shock," the doctor announces. "She needs rest, to stay warm, and keep her feet elevated. Watch her for a while to make sure she's breathing regularly. If she starts to have trouble, get her to the emergency room immediately."

Zeke sees the doctor out and I pick her back up. Lying on the couch won't keep her warm. I tell Zeke we need pillows and blankets. The best place for her is directly in front of the fire. Within minutes he's back and lays a heavy quilt on the floor. I sit down long enough to pull her directly against me and then lay us both down on our sides. Zeke surprises me by putting both our feet up.

"You were being treated for shock too." He sits back down and watches her. He's not going anywhere. It's in his eyes. He loves his daughter, and I know in that instant Doc is completely wrong about him. Mattie is the one person Zeke would die to protect.

"Daniel, I must express my gratitude to

you." The French Creole accent is heavy when he speaks. "My daughter would have died tonight if not for you, and just not tonight. Nancy tells me you were the one who found her when she was kidnapped. I owe you a debt that cannot be repaid."

"You don't owe me anything." I let my lips graze her hair. She always smells like fresh squeezed orange juice, but she drinks enough of the stuff to sweat it out.

"You love her."

"Yes."

We stare each other down, neither willing to concede. Finally, Zeke nods. "There is a problem in that. You realize this, yes?"

"My brother."

He shifts, letting his back rest against the chair he'd pushed out of the way earlier. "The boy has feelings for her, but I'm not sure how much of it is the bond they share. They could both be confusing those feelings."

"She has trust issues." I settle back down, letting her head rest on my arm. "She grew up never really knowing what it meant to be loved. Even her mom didn't love her like a parent is supposed to. Claire was a heroin addict. The drugs came first. Mattie didn't start learning what love meant until recently."

"Until she met you."

"Yes. She was used to screwing up and everyone leaving her. I didn't. She's learned to trust, that she can depend on other people, and that it's okay to care about someone else. Mary Cross is a huge part of that. She has helped Mattie learn to let people love her and to not be afraid of loving others. Mary's her sister. Maybe not by blood, but for all intents and purposes, they're sisters. I hope you're smart enough to know the kind of damage separating them would cause, especially now."

"The Cross family gave my daughter a home, a real home where she was accepted and loved. They're her family as much as I am."

I let out a grunt. One less worry off my mind.

"Do you think she has feelings for your brother?"

"She barely knows him. I think the Guardian Angel bond muddies up the waters. She has doubts about Eli's feelings for her. She thinks it's the bond, but she is willing to see what happens."

"And you?"

A sigh rumbles out. "I don't know what I'm feeling right now. I just watched my girlfriend die. Everything is too raw right now to make sense of it all."

"I am sorry about Megan."

"Thank you."

"Go to sleep, Daniel. Your eyes are drooping. I'll watch over you both. You're safe here with me."

He's right about one thing. I am tired. My body has had all it can take for the night, and I drift off to the smell of oranges, knowing Mattie is safe in my arms.

Chapter Four

Mattie

The sound of my own teeth chattering drags me out of a deep sleep. I sit up, shaking from the cold. Darkness greets me, only a faint glow of light teasing me from under what I assume is a door. A musty smell tickles my nose, like old clothes left too long in a trunk. It's not damp, and I'm pretty sure I'm standing barefoot on wood floors. Not new floors, but the clapboard style you see in a lot of attics in old houses. One of my foster homes had floors like that.

Maybe I'm dreaming.

A scuffling noise splinters the silence. *Please don't be rats, please don't be rats, please don't be rats*. One of the few fears I have is rats. I search the darkness, but find nothing. I hear it again toward my left, and I swing in that direction, but it's hard to see anything. The little fraction of light under the door doesn't penetrate more than a few inches.

The louder the sound becomes, the more I realize it's not scuffling, but *scratching*. It sounds more like something scratching against the walls. Which inspires a whole new set of concerns. I'd let Mary talk me into watching that stupid movie, *Don't Be Afraid of the Dark*. The one with all those little creatures that only came out in the dark. I hadn't been able to go into a dark room for weeks afterward. Now, thoughts of those little monsters begin to invade my subconscious, and without hesitation, I make a beeline for the door.

Something slithers across my feet, tangling around them, and I trip. Instinctively, I put my hands out in front of me to break my fall. All I manage to do is to land with all my weight on my sprained wrist, pulling a strangled cry of pain out of me.

Laughter, soft and low, echoes in the inky black depths around me. Shivers race up my arms at the hollowness of that laugh. Soulless. Empty and dark.

I sit up slowly. My eyes are finally starting to adjust, and I can make out faint shapes of what could be anything from boxes to small, scary monsters. My entire arm is throbbing in pain, and I clutch it to my chest, using my other hand to rub it.

Footsteps approach, and I snake my head in their direction. Running footsteps surround me, a little boy's laughter trailing in their wake. Only it's not a happy laugh. It's cruel, hurtful. Not a sound a child should know.

"Hello?" I whisper, getting to my knees. "Who's here?"

Fingers graze my cheek, and I flinch. His touch feels like he just stuck a hot poker to my face. Not a ghost. A ghost's energy is cold. This? This is something worse. Something I've never felt before.

"Little boy?" I stand, ready for a fight.

"Plaaay?"

The word jackknifes through my head, sending waves of blinding pain through it.

"You want to play?" I ask, my voice hoarse. What is this thing?

"Play with us."

Us? I take another look around the room. More laughter joins in. Footsteps move all through the room, some coming close to me before retreating. How many are there?

"I can't play with you if I can't see you."

Hands reach for me, tugging at my clothes, and sharp fingernails dig into my skin. I snarl at the unexpected pain. I try to run again, toward the door, but small hands grab my feet and yank, causing me to tumble forward. I land face first this time, my head bouncing off the floor.

Before I can react, they are on me, their little hands everywhere, holding me down. As hard as I struggle, I can't shake them.

"Plaaay."

I look up when I hear him right in front of me. My mind stumbles, refusing to believe what it's seeing. I blink several times, but he's still there, still smiling down at me. Even in the dark, I can see him when I can't see any of the others. That alone ratchets up my fear a notch or two. Creepy little kids are the worst.

He's maybe six or seven. Dark blond hair, whole patches of it missing from his head, hangs in a stringy mess down his face. He's not pale. No, there's color to his cheeks, but it's his eyes I can't look away from. There's no pupil, no iris, just a yellow orb flashing hatred where his eyes should be.

The odor hits me a second later. Rotten eggs…sulphur. He smells like sulphur. Only demons smell like sulphur.

He squats down in front of my face, his little hand pressing against my cheek. "Plaay?"

A full body shudder overwhelms me when he touches me. His touch is full of the dark, of pain, and rage. This child is nothing but a hollow shell that holds the promise of dark things, of horror.

"You…you want to play?" I whisper, trying to sound braver than I am. I'm terrified.

He smiles again, his teeth black and sharpened. His thumb sweeps back and forth over my cheek and then digs into the soft flesh. I hiss at the unexpected pain.

"Pretty." He leans down, and something wet and sticky plops on my cheek. It smells worse than he does. He puts his nose in my hair and sniffs. All the while, his little friends hold me down, their whispers faint and all the more terrifying because of it.

The door opens, flooding the room for a moment with bright light. It blinds me, but I can hear the gentle sobs of a child. When the door closes, the hands on me still. The entire place is as silent as a tomb.

Except for the kid who's crying.

The mood in the room shifts. I can almost taste it. They go from curious to feral in a heartbeat. I twist, trying to get loose, sensing what's coming. The fingers dig deeper into my skin, holding me tighter. I open my mouth to warn the kid, but nothing comes out. Maybe it's shock, or maybe the childlike creatures holding me did something, I don't know.

Whispers come from all corners of the room, and the little demonic child whose hand is still on my face turns toward the sound of the child sobbing. His head cocks and he listens intently. The whispers increase, and the kid crying becomes aware of it. He hiccups, and I hear him shuffle like he's sitting up or something.

"Hello?" It *is* a little boy. He sounds older than I'd thought. Maybe eight or nine, but I can't see him. It's too dark. Which only makes the fact I can see the creature still holding onto me much, much worse. Its face turns predatory; the yellow eyes pulse with glee. I keep struggling even if it's useless. I have to try to help the kid.

Footsteps, so many footsteps creeping closer, whispers and laughs mingling. The little boy cries out in pain. I can't see what's going on, but I do smell the tinny, coppery scent of blood. They must have cut him deep enough to bleed. A lot, if I can smell it.

"Yummmm." My eyes swivel up to the creature. Yum? What does that mean? Are they going to…

No! I close my eyes as they run toward the little boy, and his screams rise, blotting out every other sound. Horrible, agonizing sounds. The sounds of flesh being ripped, of bones breaking reach me and I gag, struggling to get free.

The little beast leans down and whispers in my ear, "Ready to play?"

Chapter Five

I'm assaulted by the bright rays of the sun when I shoot up, my fist connecting with something solid. I draw back again, ready to defend myself against those creepy little demonic children.

"Hey!" Dan ducks when I can't stop my fist. "What gives?"

A dream…a freaking dream. A low, nervous laugh escapes me. It was only a dream. "Sorry, bad dream."

"You came awake swinging, Squirt. Had to be more than a bad dream." He rubbed his jaw. I must have hit him before he could duck the first time.

"It was weird and freaky, and just…I don't want to talk about it." I stand and stretch. We are in my dad's office. Dan yawns and stands up himself. Did we both sleep on the floor all night? Why were we on the floor, anyway?

Before I can ask, he holds up a hand. "After your ghost visitor last night, you went into shock. Mr. Crane thought it best if you and I were both warm, so we slept down here in front of the fire, with your dad as watchdog."

Ghost visitor? I don't remember any ghost visitor. "What are you talking about?"

"The ghost...the one that attacked you in the hallway upstairs?" He runs a hand through his mussed hair, clearly confused by my lack of memory. "I saw it, Mattie. Scariest kid I've ever seen."

A kid? Maybe the same one I'd dreamed about? "What did it look like?"

"A little girl. At least I *think* it was a girl. She was battered and bruised, her eyes almost black with rage. Someone did a number on that kid."

So not the same one I'd dreamed about. Maybe they were connected? Doc would know...I shake my head. Nope, not talking to the liar about anything ever

63

again.

"Nope, Officer Dan, I got nothing." I shrug.

"What's the last thing you remember?"

"Walking back upstairs to check on you. Then…" I frown, concentrating. It's like a big empty hole is sitting there. "Then nothing."

"I guess it might be the shock…" He stops mid-sentence and steps closer to me. His finger reaches toward my cheek, and I pull away, startled.

"Do I have dirt or something on me?"

"Or something." His thumb brushes my cheek and his nose wrinkles when he pulls it away.

Black goo. He'd wiped black goo off my face. Something had fallen off the kid onto my cheek in my dream.

"Maybe it wasn't a dream."

"What?" His brown eyes are intense. He remembers the black goo the same as I do. We'd seen it before when that demon kept attacking me in New Orleans.

"The dream I had." I rub at my face and tell him about the dream.

"We should call Dr. Olivet. The only other time this happened was when you met Silas and he cut your wrist in a dream. We're out of our depth here."

"No!" I grab his arm to stop him when he reaches in his back pocket to fish out his phone. He gives me the same look he gives his dad's dog when the Yorkshire terrier tries to bully the German shepherd next door. The "why am I acting crazy" look.

"We need to talk about Doc, but not right now, okay?" I don't want to get into this with him before I get food in my belly. I'm crabbier when I'm hungry. My belly growls in agreement.

Dan rolls his eyes. "I swear you have a bottomless pit for a stomach."

"As do all the Cranes."

We both look toward the door where Zeke stands, looking tired and worn out. Had he slept at all last night?

"Mrs. Banks has prepared breakfast. She wasn't sure what you two liked, so she made a little of everything. I think we'll all need our stamina for when your grandparents arrive."

Grandparents…oh crap! I'd forgotten about that. Panic curls low in my stomach. Dan steps up behind me, wrapping an arm around me. "Breathe, Mattie." A deep calm settles over me, a calm that only Dan can inspire. He's the only person who can talk me down from a ledge.

"Food." Yep, that's what I need.

Dan snorts when my stomach lets out a growl and lets me go. We follow Zeke through the apartment into the kitchen where a breakfast nook is set up. Three places are set, a very proper placemat setting. I usually just grab a plate and sit wherever, but I don't think that's the acceptable thing to do in the Crane household. Yet another difference between us. I'm still terrified I'll embarrass Zeke because I grew up poor and he comes from old money, even though he assures me that will never happen. Even Dan looks uncomfortable at the fancy setting.

"You must be Mattie."

The loud voice comes from the woman dishing eggs out into a serving dish.

She's in her late forties, and her creamy skin sets off her dark brown eyes. Picking up the bowl, she sets it on the counter where a small mountain of food waits.

"Mattie, this is Mrs. Banks." Zeke picks up his plate and heads to the counter and starts to load it up with a variety of food. Maybe he'd seen how uncomfortable Dan and I were with the table? I'm guessing Mrs. Banks usually serves him what he wants.

"Hi." I wave a hand awkwardly in her direction. "Thanks for going out and finding us toothbrushes and clean clothes last night."

"You're welcome, honey bunny." Her smile is as bright as the warmth oozing out of her voice. Though I'm not sure about the honey bunny remark. She's not dressed like a housekeeper either. She has on jeans and a *Walking Dead* t-shirt. Not what I was expecting at all.

"Who's your favorite character?" Dan nods toward her shirt and starts to fill his own plate. He's a big fan of the show, but I've never much gotten into it. Doesn't mean he hasn't filled endless hours of my time agonizing over who he thinks may die this season.

"Lord a mercy, I just don't know." Mrs. Banks groans with real frustration. "I love them all, but I guess if you made me choose, it would be Rick, especially when he gets that crazy in his eyes."

"I'm a Daryl man, and I'm not ashamed to say it." Dan spears three pancakes. "I mean, for a guy who wasn't even in the original comics, he's morphed into a diehard fan favorite."

Zeke rolls his eyes much like I do when I've heard something a billion times and am sick to death of it. Perhaps my dad and I have more in common than I thought. Dinner table manners aside, we both are tired of hearing about this subject.

I grab my own plate and load it down with pancakes. I'm all for eggs and bacon, but you give me a choice between that and pancakes, pancakes will win every time. I snag the orange juice pitcher and bring it to the table as well. Zeke's plate is stuffed with eggs, bacon, sausage, and pancakes.

"Good morning!" Montgomery beams at us when he rolls in, newspaper in hand, which he hands over to Zeke. "It smells delicious, Mrs. Banks."

She flushes a bit, and Dan I exchange knowing glances. Someone either has a crush or is trying to hide a blooming romance. When she and Montgomery fill up their own plates and proceed to take a seat at the island, my eyebrows make a race for my hairline.

Zeke laughs. "I'm not as formal as you think, Mattie. Montgomery and Mrs. Banks usually eat breakfast in here with me every morning. Only don't tell my mother." He grimaces, a strained expression replacing his smile. "She'd have a fit."

"So she's all proper, then?" I take a bite of the homemade pancake and nearly die of food lust. I've never tasted anything so delicious in my life. She has IHOP beat, and that's my favorite place to gorge on the yumminess that is pancakes.

"Well, she was raised in a different era." Mrs. Banks comes over and refills

Zeke's coffee before sitting down. "You have to remember that. I don't fault her for it. Now, if this one here tried that nonsense, he'd end up with burned meals and no clean underwear for a month."

"Don't even threaten that!" Zeke looks horrified. It's not the kind of fake horror people use when joking. I'm betting she's made good on that in the past.

Dan isn't paying attention to either of them. He's staring at the front page of *The Charlotte Observer*. Meg's and Jake's pictures are front and center. My smile slides away, replaced by grief and a rage that spirals up from seemingly nowhere. It burns away every emotion except fury.

"Mattie?"

Zeke's voice sounds far away as I stare at the newspaper. Both dead. Because of me.

"When did her eyes start to do this?"

"It's new." Dan's voice is muffled when I flick my gaze to Mason's picture. If I could get my hands on him right now, I'd make him eat his innards as I flayed every inch of skin from his bones…

Dan's fingers snap in front of my face, and I blink. What the heck? What am I thinking? Why would I even think…it sounds more like something Silas would say. What is wrong with me?

"Hey, you okay?" Concern fills his puppy dog brown eyes.

"Yeah…yeah." I take a shaky breath. "I just wasn't expecting to see that."

Zeke's eyes flicker down to the paper. He shakes his head and flips it over. "I'm so sorry, *ma petite*. I didn't even look at it."

"It's fine." I wave his apology off before turning my attention to Dan. "Never mind me. How are you?"

I can see the grief on his face, but he's pushing it aside to focus on me. Not a good thing. Holding stuff inside is never good. A lesson I learned the hard way.

"I wasn't expecting it either." He runs a hand through his hair. "I should probably go over and see her parents."

Zeke clears his throat. "It might be a good idea to give them a few days, Daniel. They need time to grieve before the outside world invades."

I narrow my eyes. Zeke isn't telling us everything, but I'm not about to grill him in front of Dan. I have a sinking suspicion they blame both of us for their daughter's death, and in truth, they'd be right. We'd both had a hand in it, unwitting or not.

"I heard we had a visitor last night." Montgomery switches the subject. "How are you feeling this morning, Miss Mattie?"

Zeke chuckles at my expression. Lord only knows what it must look like if it's expressing any of the surprise jolting through me. "Montgomery and Mrs. Banks know all about our family. *Everything*."

The emphasis on the word *everything* makes Dan press his lips together. It's the cop in him. He can't help it. I'm fairly certain my father is a criminal. He's just good at not getting caught. Something I'm choosing to ignore for the minute.

Dan apparently decides to do the same thing, at least for now. I suspect it'll come up sooner rather than later. "She doesn't remember any of it."

"No?" Zeke sets his coffee down, startled. "Nothing?"

I shake my head. "Nada."

"That is unusual." He rubs a hand over his jawline. "Perhaps it was the shock?"

Shrugging, I guzzle down half a glass of orange juice.

"Well, perhaps it's best if you both go back to the E.R. to get checked out."

No, no, no…no more hospitals for me. Not for a very long time. "I don't need to go to the hospital. I'm fine, really."

Before Zeke can argue, Dan's phone rings. He pulls it out of his pocket. "Sorry. I have to take this. It's my dad. I'll be right back." He gets up and goes into the other room.

"Mattie." The hesitancy in Zeke's voice raises my hackles. I am so not going to lose this fight over the hospital. Nope, not going back there. "When did your eyes start going black?"

My breath whooshes out. Is that what happened to me earlier? When the rage took over?

"I…"

"I just want to help, Mattie, but I have

to understand what's going on."

Usually, I'd talk to Doc about this, but that's no longer an option. Maybe trusting Zeke isn't a bad idea. "When we found Dan at his apartment, almost dead, something broke inside me. I went cold. The world turned dark, and everything got stripped away. There was nothing left but fear and anger. The thought of losing him was too much, and this door opened in my mind. Whatever was behind it burned away everything but the anger. It gave me the strength I needed to hold onto Dan and make Silas save him."

"You made Silas save him?" Zeke's consternation was plain in his voice. "Mattie, you can't make a demon do anything. You barter with them."

"Silas said he owed me a freebie, and I used it on Dan. I also told him if he let Dan die, I would see him dead."

Zeke let out a slow breath. "Mattie...they don't do freebies either."

I held up my hands. "He healed my hands too."

"At what price?"

"None. He didn't ask for anything."

"I don't understand." Zeke sweeps his eyes over me. "He asked for nothing?"

"Not a thing." I shrug, as confused about it as Zeke. Eli had told me the same thing. Demons don't do anything for free, but he'd asked nothing of me.

"Silas has taken a very unusual interest in you." Zeke swallows the last of his coffee. "It's disturbing, especially given the way your eyes just changed."

"Why?"

His lips thin. "Only a demon's eyes go black, Emma Rose."

Fudgepops. And he'd used my real name. "Are you saying I'm a demon?"

"No." His words are firm. "If you were a demon, you couldn't set foot in this house. It's warded against demons and angels. Neither of those beings can enter."

He had his home warded against angels? "Angels?"

He sighed. "Angels are not the beings you think they are, *ma petite*. Some are, but most are not. They are just as devious as demons in some ways."

"But…angels are supposed to be

good."

"Angels are complicated." He stands and picks up his plate, walking over to the sink. "There is a lot you must learn, *ma petite*, and now is not the time to get into that discussion. Let's concentrate on your eyes, *oui*?"

Sure. Let's focus on the fact that I might be exhibiting demonic tendencies instead of talking about angels being bad guys. Neither option appeals to me.

"Can you give us a few minutes alone?" Zeke puts his plate in the sink. I pay little heed to Montgomery and Mrs. Banks when they both leave the room. The only thing I see is the growing anger on my father's face.

"I don't think Silas saved Daniel for free." Zeke leans against the sink, his arms crossed. "I think he got exactly what he wanted."

"Which is?"

"There is something you must know about your family." Anger wars with concern in his expression. "Not the Cranes. Even we draw the line at some things."

"But not my mother's family?" I clench my hands, dread curling in the pit of my stomach. I know what he's going to say.

"I don't know if it's true or not." He walks back to the table and sits in the empty seat next to me. Taking my hand, he looks me straight in the eyes. "It's something that has been whispered about in our circles for over a century, and it may just be that—rumors."

"Just spit it out, Zeke." I can't take all this beating around the bush. Just tell me already.

"It's rumored that they've bred with demons."

My stomach bottoms out. Vertigo. Everything starts to spin out of control as the world around me crashes into nothingness. Empty. Hollow. I *am* a demon.

"Mattie…if you were really a demon, you couldn't enter this house."

"What if my human half cancels that out?" I whisper. "Have you ever accounted for that in any of your wards?"

"Yes."

The finality in his voice brings my eyes up to his face, hope springing to life.

"Our family deals in demons, Emma Rose. We don't hide that fact, and we prepare for any and all eventualities, including the rumors of witches and other supernaturals breeding with demons. The wards protecting us take that into account."

"Then what did you mean when you said Silas got what he wanted?"

"Just because you aren't a demon, doesn't mean you can't have inherited some traits. Perhaps he's interested in you because he knows of a specific trait your mother's family possesses. Maybe he's been trying to get you to find that part of yourself and open up to it. Perhaps Daniel put you in the right frame of mind to access whatever that is."

"But it still means…"

"No, it doesn't make you a demon." He leans closer, his eyes bright. "And even if you were half demon, you're still *my* daughter, and I love you. That will *never* change, Emma Rose. I swear it."

And oddly, I believed him. Despite

everything crashing around me, that simple truth bleeding from his eyes comfort me. But what about everyone else? Dan…Eli.

Before I can say anything, Dan bursts into the room, his eyes bright, almost fevered.

"What is it?" What new shoe is about to drop?

"Jake's not dead."

Chapter Six

"I need to stop at Mary's."

"You've never called Mary's home." Dan shifts into the right lane so he can take the exit ahead that goes to the Cross' neighborhood. He'd borrowed one of Zeke's cars since his truck was still in the parking lot of his apartment complex.

"I've never called anywhere home." Mary and her mom are great, best foster home ever, and they accept me for who I am, ghost abilities and all. But they're not home, not really. I don't belong to them. For me, home is a sense of belonging to the people there. Maybe I'm wrong in that respect, but it's an old ingrained idea from being in foster care where I got shipped from home to home.

It's something I want to change, though. Since meeting Dan, he's been teaching me there are different types of families. He's family to me. And I guess maybe I do belong to him in that sense. I shake my head. My thoughts are so scattered.

It's the elephant in the back seat with us, I guess. Neither one of us wants to talk about it, but my mind keeps going there.

Jake.

Part of me is so happy, but part of me is a little shell-shocked. Dan's dad called to tell him he'd spoken to Mrs. Owens, and she's hopeful I will come by the hospital. I don't want to go.

I know what happened wasn't Jake's fault, and I don't blame him at all. His brother was a crazy psycho. Just the thought of being around him, though, makes me think about Mason and Paul and everything they did to us. Then to face their mom? I can't. I just can't.

But I have to.

Dan and Zeke both agreed I didn't have to. But how can I not? His mom is one of the nicest people I know. She'd taken me in and treated me so kindly while Jake and I were together. How can I not repay that kindness?

"About your dad…"

I look over to see Dan chewing on his bottom lip, something he does when he's nervous.

"Yeah, what about Zeke?"

"He's not like I thought he'd be." He turns the heat up, shivering. Odd. I'm the one who's usually cold in the blazing Carolina heat. It has to be over ninety outside already, but to me it feels lukewarm. Maybe he's still suffering some of the side effects of shock. Keeping a shock victim warm is important.

"Me either. After everything everyone said about him, I was expecting some creepy, cold monster of a man, but he's not. At least not with me. And he has a pretty cool accent."

"I think maybe you can call his place home."

My head snaps back around to look at him. Did he just say what I think he said? I mean, Dan's the first person to jump up and shout caution in big red warning letters when it comes to Zeke, but now he wants me to call Zeke's home? What in the world happened last night while I was out?

Not that Zeke would object. He wants me to stay with him. Truthfully, I think he wants to whisk me off to New Orleans. Part of me wants to go, to get away from every bad thing that's ever happened to me. It would be a truly new beginning for me with people who wanted me.

Then I think about Dan. I almost lost him. The fear is fresh enough to make my lungs close up and my heart shift into overdrive remembering those dark hours. He matters to me. More than anyone, more than Mary, more than Zeke, even more than Eli. He's Officer Dan.

My life would be so much easier if I could go back to the old Mattie, the girl who didn't have people to worry or care about. The girl before Dan Richards.

"He wants me to come to New Orleans."

"You aren't going." The steel in his

voice shocks me. "Neither of us know him well enough to trust him."

"Dan, you just said I could call his place home."

"That's here in Charlotte where I can watch him." Anger laces every word he bites out.

"What if I want to go?" My voice is soft and hesitant. "Would you come with me?"

He stares at me, his eyes unreadable.

"Watch the road, Officer Dan."

His eyes snap back to the highway, but he doesn't say a word. Instead, he turns in to my neighborhood. I look out the window, trying to figure out how to laugh off that last question. I shouldn't have asked it. I should have kept my big mouth shut. I'd blurted it out without thinking. Of course he can't go with me. I mean, he's got to stay here for his mom's trial. He just found the Malones. They moved here to Charlotte so they could get to know him. I can't ask him to walk away from all that.

The neighborhood's quiet today, but they have some big community event going on at one of the parks downtown. Lots are probably down there and the rest are most likely in church. It's Sunday morning and early yet.

As we pull into Mary's drive, I see Kayla playing in her yard next door. She's Mr. Burnett's seven-year-old granddaughter. She and her mom moved in with him last month. Bad divorce or something. She's a cute kid, though. Blonde pigtails bounce as she hops from one place to another, and big old sky blue eyes twinkle with laughter. I wave to her when I get out and she grins, her teddy bear dragging the ground by one hand as she waves back. She has two teeth missing, making her cute factor skyrocket. My eyes drop to her old, scrappy bear. I don't think I've ever seen her without that old thing. Kids.

Mary comes barreling out the house, almost knocking me over when she wraps me in a bear hug. I think we both might have fallen if Dan hadn't steadied me. I laugh at her obvious delight. She still reminds me of a big ball of sunshine with all that blonde hair.

"Don't you dare laugh!" She hits me in the arm. "There is nothing to laugh about. Do you know how scared I was? Then you didn't come home and you weren't answering any of my texts or messages. I was freaking out all night, worried about you. Mattie, you almost died last night. There is nothing to laugh about."

My laughter dies as her tears sober me up. I guess I've gotten so used to "almost dying" over the last year, it feels normal to me. I shouldn't have laughed. Mary doesn't have my crazy life. None of this is normal to her.

"I'm sorry." I pull her back into a hug. "I was laughing because you are always so happy to see me. It just made me smile, that's all. I didn't mean to upset you."

"Fine, apology accepted. Just don't do that again, Mattie. When I call you after a near death experience, pick up the phone."

"I promise."

She glares at me for another hot minute before deciding to forgive me. "Mom's in the kitchen baking blueberry muffins.

She knows you love them. Come on."

We follow her into the house, and after much the same reaction from her mom, Mrs. Cross sits us all down at the kitchen table with fresh muffins. My stomach growls merrily as the smell hits my nose. I can eat even when I'm full. I mean, who am I to let all that baking go to waste?

"Your social worker called." Mrs. Cross snaps the Tupperware container shut and puts the rest of the muffins on the counter. "She couldn't reach you either last night or this morning."

Oops. I'm so gonna hear it from Nancy when she finally catches up with me. She's the absolute best social worker ever, even if she does have a crush on Zeke.

"I'll call her on the way to the hospital." The sweet smell of fresh muffins tickles my nose as I lean down and inhale.

"Hospital?" Alarm spreads on Mrs. Cross's face. "Why are you going to the hospital?"

"To see Jake."

"Jake?" Mary frowns at me, clearly

unaware of the latest development.

Dan explains the situation while I eat my muffin. "We are also going to swing by the Malones' place too. I promised we'd come over later this afternoon. I think Heather is going to thump us all if she can't meet Mattie soon."

"Wait...my grandparents are arriving." I swallow the last bite. "Maybe we should put off seeing the Malones until tomorrow."

"I forgot about that." Dan leans back, thinking. "Maybe we can go see them before the hospital, and that way we have a great excuse for not staying long?"

"Is this about me, or you not having to spend time over there?" I grill him with my best Officer Dan patented stare.

He looks uncomfortable, but merely stares back, his Officer Dan stare much, much better than mine. Dang it. How does he do it so well?

"How are you supposed to get to know them if you don't spend time with them?" I push my plate toward Mary, who's getting up to put her own plate in the sink. She grabs it without question.

Still nothing from him.

"They all sat there by your bedside while you were in the hospital. I think that earns them some points in the family department, especially Ava. She refused to leave the hospital till you woke up."

His eye twitches at the mention of his baby sister.

"They moved here, Dan, no questions asked, because you were here. They're trying. So hard."

"I know that." The words burst out of him. "I just…my mom…how can I face them all after what she did? I mean, being forced to be around Eli and Caleb when they're here is one thing, but going over there and just spending time with them for the sake of it? I don't know if I can do that."

"You can." I grab his hand and the heat seeps into me. "You can because it's the right thing to do for everyone. They're your family, Dan. Don't turn your back on that. Family is the most important thing in the world. Even families that come about in an unorthodox manner."

"When did you get to be Dr. Phil?" His

smile is barely there, but it's there.

"When you taught me what the true meaning of family is." I lean over the table and kiss his cheek. His eyes glow with warmth when I finally look into them, my face only an inch from his. Something passes between us, some undefinable emotion that cements us together for eternity. "You can do this because I'll be there. We'll get through it together."

"Awww," Mary coos at us. "Hallmark moment!"

Dan laughs and the moment passes. I sit back in my chair, and an uneasy feeling crawls over my skin that has nothing to do with Dan. It's strange. I stand and walk into the front room, looking over everything, but nothing is out of place. Just this weird feeling.

"Mattie, you okay?" Mary asks, coming in behind me.

"Yeah, but I don't know…"

"What?" Dan is right behind her.

A loud banging on the front door makes me jump. I swing my gaze to it as Mrs. Cross answers the door. Dana,

Kayla's mother, is standing there terrified and half-crazed.

My bad feeling turns to true fear at the words she utters before bursting into tears.

"Kayla's gone. I can't find her anywhere!"

Chapter Seven

Dan

The panic-stricken mother falls to the floor, tears streaming as hysterical sobs overtake her. I know her, not by name, but I've seen her next door a few times when I'd come over here. The little girl who'd been playing earlier is her daughter. The most likely story is the little girl is at a friend's house or just walked a little too far out of her mother's shouting range. But with so many children gone missing over the last few weeks, I'm not about to take any chances.

"Dan, do something." Mary's eyes are wide, panicked, but Mattie looks almost resigned. She's thinking along the same lines I am.

"Ma'am." I approach her slowly, not wanting to upset her more than she already is. "I'm Officer Dan Richards. Why don't we go into the kitchen, get you some water, and then you tell me what happened?"

She hiccups, but lets Mrs. Cross help her off the floor and into the kitchen. I turn to Mary and Mattie. "Go look outside. Knock on every door and check for anything out of the ordinary. Check three blocks in each direction, then hightail it back here with your report." Neither says a word as they run out the door. One task down.

I pull out my phone and call the station. I give them my name and badge number and ask for assistance at the address in handling a missing child case, possible abduction. Once I've done all that, I go back into the kitchen and sit across from the distraught mother, who keeps trying to get up and go out and search for her child.

"I have Mattie and Mary out looking for her now." I keep my voice calm and steady as I pull up the recorder app on my phone and press record. "I know you're scared, but I have people out looking for your little girl. I have more officers on the way to help search. The best thing you can do right now is help me understand what happened. Can you do that for me?"

"I...I..." She closes her cobalt blue eyes, tears making wet tracks down her makeup sodden cheeks. "I'll try."

"Okay." I give her a reassuring smile. "What's your name?"

"Amber." She takes a deep, steadying breath. "Amber Rawlins."

I grab a paper towel, thankful we'd left them on the table earlier, and the pen Mrs. Cross hands me and start jotting down notes. "What's your little girl's name, Mrs. Rawlins?"

"Kayla. She's only six. I should be out there..."

"And you will be. I just need some information first. What was Kayla wearing?"

"Shorts and her Disney princess shirt." She picks up the glass of water, some of it sloshing over the rim as her hand shakes. "She's been grumpy since she woke up, and my head was pounding, and I told her to go outside for a while…" A sob breaks from her and the glass falls, breaking when it hits the tile floor.

"What color were her shorts?" I pull her out of her blame and back to what's important. Blaming herself for having a headache isn't going to help anyone.

"White…she always wears them with her princess shirt."

Mrs. Cross starts to clean up the mess on the floor, and Amber notices all the broken glass. "I'm so sorry!" She tries to get down and help, but I reel her back to the description of her daughter.

"What about her princess shirt? What color was it?"

"Yellow." The words tumble out absently as she stares at the front door. She has a clear line of sight from where we are sitting. "Belle. She loves *Beauty and the Beast*. Why did I get so frustrated and send her out to play?" Her tears start up again. "We have to find her."

"Does Kayla have any scars or birthmarks?" I ask instead of telling her we'll find the girl. I refuse to make a promise I can't keep. Never promise a parent they'll find their missing child. It's one of the first lessons I'd learned from my partner.

"What...no...yes. She wrecked her bike last summer. Split her knee wide open. It left a jagged scar."

"Which knee?" I can hear police sirens in the distance. Backup. I keep the relief off my face. She needs to see only calm reassurance.

"I don't remember." She clasps her hands together to try and still their trembling. "I should remember that. What kind of mother doesn't remember that?"

"A scared one." Mrs. Cross wraps an arm around the woman's shoulder. "You're a good mother, Amber. You're just scared and in shock right now. Just try to stay calm and let the police do their job."

Several loud knocks pound on the door, and I get up to answer it. They've gotten here faster than I'd thought. Detective Brody of Robbery Homicide waits on the other side. He nods briskly, his brown eyes grim as I give him a rundown on everything I've learned before we go back into the kitchen. I tap his shoulder when he sits and point to my phone. He gives me a nod of approval.

"Amber, this is Detective Brody. He's here to help. He's going to ask you some questions."

"Where are you going?" Panic resurfaces in her eyes.

"I'm going to go outside and give the other officers Kayla's description, then I'm going to start searching for her myself."

She nods, her movement wooden despite the glassy look of fear in her eyes. I waste no time in escaping. As soon as I hit the front porch, I let out the breath I've been holding. There's this nasty feeling in my gut I'd squashed while questioning her, but now it bubbles over.

"Hey, Dan."

I see Chris Jenkins, an officer from my

academy class, coming up the drive. He's my age and we've been friends for a while.

"You caught the case?" He stops just as I step down.

"Accident. I brought Mattie over, and…"

"Right time, right place, huh?"

That's an understatement. I motion for him to follow me, and we walk over to the police officers setting up a perimeter. More squad cars are arriving, as well as the CMPD mobile unit. Anything involving the disappearance of a child under ten is considered a critical missing. We don't say a missing child in this situation, instead we all refer to it as a critical missing. Helps people to stay focused and not panic. The street might look like chaos at the moment, but it's an organized chaos.

My captain, Sheila Warner, steps out of the mobile command unit. In her late forties, her brown hair is starting to show signs of silver, but her blue eyes remain sharp as ever. She looks around, and when her gaze lands on me, she frowns. I know what she's thinking. I've taken a leave of absence, which means I'm not on active duty. I'm still a cop, though, out of uniform or not.

Another detective I don't know takes my statement and gets a description of the little girl and what she was last seen wearing for an Amber Alert. As soon as I'm done, Captain Warner is waiting for me.

"Dan."

"I know I'm not…"

She holds up a hand to stop me. "You did good, Dan. I just spoke with Brody. He says you had the good sense to record your conversation, and we've got enough to get out a good description over the wire. I'm not going to bust your chops for not being on active duty. It's all hands on deck when we have a missing child. Especially right now."

I can see Mary and Mattie running back toward me. They skid to a halt a minute later. Both are shaking their heads, and the heavy pit in my stomach only gets worse.

"Nobody's seen her." Mary wheezes as

she tries to catch her breath. "We knocked on every door just like you said."

"Captain, this is Mary Cross and Mattie Hathaway. Guys, this is my police captain, Sheila Warner."

"The infamous Mattie Hathaway." Despite the situation, I see a twinkle in her eye when Mattie attempts not to squirm. Mattie and the police have had several run-ins over the last few years. The girl has a rap sheet most cons would be proud of. She and Detective Brody are on a first name basis, if I remember correctly.

Mattie narrows her eyes, and before she can say any of her patented snarky comebacks, I turn to Mary. "Did you guys notice anything unusual in the neighborhood?"

Mary shakes her head. "No. Most people aren't even home."

"Captain! We found something!"

We all turn to look when someone shouts from the Rawlins house. The officer stares at the ground, grim as death. Whatever he found can't be at all good.

Captain Warner is across the street faster than I can blink. The woman can move in those heels. It reminds me of Meg. She could always run faster than me, even in her heels…a dizzying sensation swims up when I remember she's gone.

Mattie's hand slips into mine and she leans into me. Her hand is cool to the touch, but it's comforting. She knows me too well. Mary looks like she's about to say something, and I drag Mattie with me and follow the captain. I can't deal with any condolences. I haven't even had time to come to grips with Meg's death yet. Until I do, it's best to focus on something else.

And right now, the most important thing is finding Kayla. Alive.

That thought gets beaten down when I see what everyone is staring at.

An older model Buick sedan is parked on the street in front of the Rawlins house. I'd seen it when we pulled up earlier, but I hadn't paid it any mind. I know the car. It belongs to one of the neighbors who works second shift and usually parks where he can when he gets home late. Mary had told me about it when I'd seen it parked in front of her house once.

Sticking out from under the front tire is a worn and faded teddy bear, its black, glassy eyes staring at us. The same teddy bear Kayla had been clutching earlier. Its ear has a wet, red stain. Smaller drops of the same substance surround it haphazardly.

No one needs to say what the bloody teddy bear means.

She's not at a friend's house or hiding from her mom.

She's gone.

***

My feet are finally starting to ache. We've all walked for miles, banging on doors, stopping people on sidewalks and outside of storefronts with our photo of Kayla Rawlins. No one has seen the girl, but I didn't expect anything else. A bloody teddy bear left behind speaks volumes about her manner of abduction. As the day wears on, my hope of finding the little girl alive fades.

Mattie hasn't said much of anything for over an hour. She's too quiet. "You okay, Squirt?"

"We're not going to find her, are we?"

"I don't know." No point in trying to reassure her. I know she has a soft spot for the little girl, and giving her false hope would only hurt her more in the end.

"I've read enough of your police books to know the longer she's gone, the less likely we are to find her alive."

The truth is the average for a missing kid is about three hours. If we haven't found them in that time frame, the less likely we are to find them alive. Not that we tell parents that, but it's an ugly truth. When I think about that bloody bear, my hope of finding the child alive gets crushed. She was taken by violence. It speaks volumes about the kind of monster who took her. If I let myself think about what she might be going through right now...I shake my head, forcing the images and thoughts out of my head. No good can come from that frame of mind. I just wish we had better news for her mother.

"I wish I could tell you we're going to find her." I stuff my hands into my pockets as we walk.

"I know." She lets out a sigh deep enough to hold the world's sorrows. It's something she does when she starts thinking about her own past, being shipped from foster home to foster home. At times like these, I want to pull her into a hug and tell her it's all going to be okay, but Mattie knows that's not the truth. She knows it better than most.

We turn the corner onto her street. The police cars have thinned out a bit, but the mobile command unit is still parked front and center. Mary and her mother are sitting on Mr. Burnette's front porch, the older man in one of the rocking chairs. He looks stricken at the loss of his granddaughter, his face drawn and showing his age in the deep wrinkle lines outlining the frown he's wearing. None of this can be good for a man of his age. As we get closer, I can see him holding a stuffed pony. Probably another favorite toy of Kayla's.

"Anything?" Mr. Burnett looks up hopefully, and I feel terrible to have to shake my head. The defeat on his face is heartbreaking.

"We're doing everything we can, sir."

"Why don't we go inside, and I'll make you a cup of tea?" Mrs. Cross gets up off the porch swing and heads toward the front door. "It'll do you some good."

Mr. Burnett nods and stands, the pony tumbling from his hand, and follows Mrs. Cross inside. The stuffed pink horse has stains on it, probably from being dragged around and from tea parties. I bend over and pick it up. It shouldn't be on the ground. It reminds me too much of the bear.

My fingers clutch the plush animal, the velvety fur soft to the touch. An image floats up, of Kayla hugging it to her chest. More and more images flicker through my mind, blinding me to the outside world. Of the little girl sitting in her room surrounded by her toys, playing like she's the queen holding court. I see her in a car, crying because her arm hurts from a shot. They roll behind my eyes faster and faster, blurring so much I can't decipher them. A sharp pain starts behind my left eye and quickly blooms to a full-on assault that feels like someone gleefully stabbing me in the eye with a rusty nail.

"*Dan!*"

Mattie's voice breaks through the kaleidoscope of images. I drop the pony and the bombardment stops. Blinking, I stumble from the fallen toy. What was that?

"What's wrong?" Mattie's eyes are wide. "What happened?"

"I...I'm not...sure." Part of me wants to pick the cursed thing back up and see if it happens again, but the other part is shaking its head. Hands up and back away slowly. I repeat the same words to myself as I would to a suspect. The animal is suspect right now. I'm not sure what it did to me.

"Dan, you look like someone just

asked you to swallow a live slug." Mattie puts her hands on her hips, irritated. "Now spit it out. What happened just now?"

Instead of answering her, I stare at the innocent looking stuffed toy. It's just lying there on the porch, staring blindly upward. I squat and reach for it, but hesitate. What if it happens again? What is "it," anyway?

"Dan?" Mattie sounds more irritated than before. I don't pay it any mind. She does that when she's worried. Once people get used to her, they understand that.

"When I picked it up earlier, I saw stuff."

"Stuff?" Mary gets on her knees beside me. "What kind of stuff?"

"Random stuff, I guess. It was like a bunch of home movies all shoved onto one tape playing really fast. All of it was Kayla, every image of her. It got so jumbled my head started to spin."

Mary's gasp made me look away from the pony. "What?"

"I think I might know what it is." Mary

jumps up and glances around. The place is still crawling with cops and reporters. "Come on, let's go back to the house."

Mattie doesn't say anything to either of us. She just turns and walks off the porch and to the Cross'.

"What's going on with her?" Mary falls into step beside me. "She seems off."

Something *is* wrong with Mattie, something more than what happened last night. She's been in a funk since we'd stopped to pick up her stuff. She'd brushed it off as a ghost, but now I'm not so sure. Or maybe she's just now beginning to process the last twenty-four hours.

"She's been through a lot." I slow down as we walk. "We got a call that Jake's not dead, too. Then Kayla…" I shake my head. "Is it any wonder she's not herself?"

"I guess." Mary chews at her lip and stops before we reach the gate. "How are you? You went through a lot too, the last couple days."

I shrug, my head ducking a bit. "I'm

dealing."

"Yeah, I get that, but you lost your girlfriend, Dan. I know Mattie had a hard time with you dating Meg, and I wasn't that supportive either, but you loved her. If you need anything, please let me know what I can do for you."

"Thanks, Mary." I give her a half-hearted smile that's probably more of a grimace, but I close the gate behind us and start up the front porch steps. I'm not ready to talk about Meg yet.

We wander into the kitchen to find Mattie pulling cans of Coke out of the fridge. She's bypassed OJ and gone straight for her sugar addiction.

"So what's wrong with Dan?" She hands us each a can and plops down on one of the island's bar stools.

"Well, I think it's kinda like what happened to me." Mary opens her can and takes a tiny sip. She's not a big Coca Cola fan. I remember when Mattie informed me of that little fact. She'd been completely flabbergasted, convinced everyone was addicted to sugar like she is. To be fair, she'd gotten me addicted to

Coke. I drink at least a can a day, much to my mom's horror.

"I don't understand." Mattie swivels in her chair so she's facing us.

"Well, Dr. Olivet can explain it better than I can, but when you are close to death and almost cross over, you can come back with certain abilities."

"You mean your ability to hear ghosts?" Mattie raises her eyebrow in question.

"Yeah, exactly like that. Maybe Dan came back a little bit psychic. I've read documented cases where people came back from near death experiences with gifts like he's describing. They're able to hold something of someone's and see things about them."

What the... "I am not psychic."

"Dan, you were on the ghost plane for a long time, close to the Between." Mattie frowns, thinking. "It's possible. I mean, you can't argue Mary hears ghosts."

Well, yes, I can, but I won't. I think Mary might want to hear them so she thinks she does. She needs therapy more than she needs me agreeing with nonsense. Just admitting ghosts are real is a big leap for me. If I hadn't seen it firsthand, I'd never have believed it.

"I'm not psychic." No way, no how. I am not a bigger freak than I already am. Seeing ghosts that have gone mad is more than enough for me. Touching things and getting a sneak peek into someone's life? No. I refuse to accept it.

"Then you explain what happened when you picked up that toy." Mattie crosses her arms over her chest and smiles expectantly.

My lips purse. I can't explain it, and she knows it.

"That's what I thought." She smirks, and I narrow my eyes. "Don't bug out. It's not that bad."

Not that bad? She's lost her marbles if she thinks seeing things in my head isn't that bad. Maybe it's the head wound? I did leave the hospital against doctor's orders. I probably need another CT scan or something. Hallucinations. That's it. I'm just hallucinating because of swelling or bleeding in the brain. That's the most rational explanation for what happened.

"Maybe we should just call Dr. Olivet?" Mary suggests.

"No."

We both stare at Mattie in disbelief. The sharp hardness of her tone speaks volumes. Why doesn't she want to talk to the doctor?

"Okay, enough is enough." I mimic her and fold my arms. "What's up with you not wanting to talk to Dr. Olivet?"

She gets that defensive, defiant look in her eyes, but I see the hurt and the fear underneath it. If you don't know her as well as I do, you'd miss it. Mary's missed it.

"I don't want to talk about it."

"Tough." I give her my best cop look, and she squirms. I need something to distract me from the possibility of some weird ability I've just inherited or a possible relapse of my brain injury. Nope, not thinking about it.

"He's a liar."

Now, that's not what I expected her to say. "What do you mean?"

She doesn't look happy about it, but

Mattie launches into the events of last night, of finding Dr. Olivet waiting on her and of the photo she'd found in his possession. He'd known who she was all along? No wonder she's pissed. Mattie hates being deceived. Once you lose her trust, it's nearly impossible to get it back. I'm still surprised she forgave me for keeping things from her. But I guess that's what the two of us do. We forgive each other, no matter what.

"He has a point." Mattie's glare swings to Mary. "Well, he does."

Mary's right. Had he come right out and told Mattie who he was, she'd never have trusted him. It's just who she is. The girl has serious trust issues.

"Would you have listened to him?" I keep my voice steady, calm. "If he'd told you that day he knew who you were, knew your mom, would you have listened, or stalked away like you usually do?"

The anger in her eyes burns brighter. She knows we're right, but she's not ready to admit it yet.

"That's not the point."

"Yeah, Squirt, it kinda *is* the point." I brace my feet, ready for a fight. "Dr. Olivet has done nothing but help you and be there for you. If he had nefarious plans for you, I think he'd have done it by now. He dropped everything and flew down here because he was afraid of what your father might do. Your mom trusted him, Mattie. Don't you think maybe you should give him a chance to explain himself? He's not a bad guy. Sure, he kept something from you, but it wasn't out of malice."

She looks like she wants to argue, but something flickers in her eyes and they flash black for the barest hint of a second. I've seen them do that before. What's caught my attention is there was an undertone of yellow in them. If I'd blinked, I'd have missed it. We really need to talk to the doctor about her eyes. I'm worried. From what Caleb's told me, only demons have black eyes. Add in the creepy yellow, and I'm more than worried. I'm scared. What did she give up in order to save me?

"Look, just think about it, okay?" I run

a hand through my hair. It's getting longer than I normally keep it. "We don't have to make a decision right now."

Her face morphs from righteous indignation to concern. "Dan, your nose is bleeding."

What? I swipe at my nose, and sure enough, when I pull it back, blood covers my fingertips. I look up, shocked and scared. What the heck is going on?

Chapter Eight

Mattie

My footsteps echo around me as I pace up and down the waiting room. What's wrong with him? Why is his nose bleeding? It hadn't stopped the entire ride here. Mary had driven us to the hospital, her mom wanting to stay with Mr. Burnett and his daughter while they waited for news of Kayla.

I knew we should have taken him back to the hospital last night. I knew it. Why did I let Zeke talk me into waiting? I can't lose him. I just can't.

The antiseptic smell that bathes all hospitals keeps tickling my nose. I hate hospitals. Nothing good ever comes out of being here. Bloody ghosts everywhere. I've already seen no fewer than six of the buggers. All trying to get my attention. Mary gave up trying to ignore them and walked outside. At least she can't see them. Two of them are gross—car accident victims, maybe? They are all banged up, one's head split open, a large chunk of glass embedded in the wound.

"Excuse me, dear?"

I stop pacing and turn to face the elderly lady who's been sitting in the waiting room chair, knitting. She's probably in her seventies, her white hair soft and perfectly done up in a bun at the back of her head. Large green eyes stare at me from behind her glasses. Someone's grandmother.

"Do you mind not pacing? You're starting to make me dizzy." Her tone is kind, so I bite back the snarky comment. I merely nod and walk down the hallway. I'll go pace where she can't see me. I need to be moving. If I sit still, this all becomes too much.

Why is his nose bleeding?

The long hallway is empty, for the

most part. I see two nurses at the end of the hall talking to each other. Or maybe one or both are lab techs. They all wear scrubs, so it's hard to tell them apart.

When they enter the set of double doors a few minutes later, it leaves me completely alone. Dan asked me not to call anyone until we know. He doesn't want to worry his parents. They've been through enough already. Not that I could call anyone. My phone is still in my purse at the banquet hall, unless Zeke had someone retrieve it.

I stop pacing and lean against the wall. My stomach is rioting, and I may end up puking soon if someone doesn't come out and tell me what's going on with Dan. Why didn't I make Zeke take him back to the hospital last night?

Sliding down the wall, I sit and wrap my arms around my legs, resting my head on my knees. I feel helpless, and I hate it. He has to be all right.

The sound of shuffling feet catches my attention, and when I look up, I see Eli Malone striding down the hall toward me, his face intent. My own personal

Guardian Angel. He looks like one with his scruffy blond hair and aqua eyes. Such beautiful eyes. Dangerous eyes. I've seen those eyes on the man who killed me in one of my visions. Even knowing this, he doesn't inspire panic, only a sense of calm. I need that calm right now.

"Hilda." He sits down beside me, resting his head against mine. He'd shortened my name Mathilda to Hilda just to annoy me. "You should have called me. I've been worried."

"I…I don't have my phone." My words are barely above a whisper. Heat seeps into me. I'm always so cold, except when I'm around Eli. He becomes my own personal furnace. According to the lore, my Guardian Angel becomes whatever I need him to be, and that's usually a furnace. I have so much ghost energy, I'm always freezing. "How did you know I was here?"

"I can always find you, Hilda. Guardian Angel bond, remember?" He wraps an arm around me and pulls me closer, his lips grazing over my cheek. "Always."

Eli is an enigma to me. He makes me feel things I have never felt. I like him. I do. A lot. But part of me wonders if it's not this freaky bond we share that has us all twisted up. Can I really trust what I feel, or is it the bond making me feel like this?

Right now, I don't really care about any of it. I just want someone to tell me it's all going to be okay, and being in Eli's arms is just as good as.

"Dan's going to be fine." His whisper reaches my ear seconds after my last thought. "Everything's going to be okay. I don't think that reaper wants to tangle with you again."

It's the bond. What I needed to hear was the first thing out of his mouth. I know it deep in my heart, but I'm selfish. I twist and curl into him and let my head rest on his chest. Eli feels so comfortable, like we've known each other forever. Maybe we have. Maybe that's why I keep dreaming of people with his eyes.

"Caleb's waiting for an update for us now. I think the nurse said they'd taken him to CT, but she was going to check on it for us."

I nod, not trusting my voice. I'm barely holding myself together. Scotch tape and Elmer's glue. Poke too hard, and I'll come apart. Out of the corner of my eye, I see the old lady who'd been sitting in the waiting room watching us. She's staring like she wants to say something, but her manners won't let her interrupt. I wonder if my grandmother will be anything like her. Sweet, kind, and totally loveable.

"Hey." He nudges the top of my head with his chin. "Talk to me, Mattie."

"Dan thinks I'm overreacting." I need to talk about something besides Dan possibly dying again. Head wounds and nose bleeds go hand in hand. Mrs. Cross had been so freaked out she'd insisted we go to the hospital on the spot. Mary's mom is a nurse, and a very good one.

"He's not dying, Hilda." Eli snuggles me closer.

"No, not about that. About Doc."

"Doc?"

I tell him about last night, about the photo. "He's known who I was all along,

Eli, and he never said a word. He lied to me for months. How am I supposed to trust him now? And the look in his eyes…it scared me."

"I've known the doc for a long time, but what he did, that's not cool, Hilda. He should have come clean with you once you'd gotten to know him. I can understand a few weeks, but months? Not cool."

"I know, right?" I shake my head. "But Dan and Mary think I'm overreacting. I've been thinking about it, and maybe they're right. Had he told me the truth right off the bat, I probably would have walked away from him. Back then, I didn't trust anyone, not even Dan. He wouldn't let me walk away from him. I tried, but he never gave up on me."

Please be okay. Please be okay. Please be okay.

"So let me guess, Mary and Dan think you should talk to the doc and let him explain himself, huh?"

"Yeah."

"Sounds like a Caleb move. He's always the rational one. Me, I'd have punched him. I'm surprised you didn't."

"Me too." A hollow laugh escapes. "I blame it on the shock."

"Don't stress about it. When you're ready to talk to the doc, you will."

"Thanks, Eli."

"So besides rushing my brother to the hospital, what else have you been up to? I tried calling last night and again this morning, but it went straight to voicemail. I even thought about coming over to check on you, but I got the feeling last night your father didn't want anyone near you."

"He's protective."

Eli snorts at the thought. I know he doesn't like Zeke, so I change the subject. "A little girl went missing from Mary's neighborhood today. I knew her. Good kid. We spent all morning searching for her. It doesn't look good."

"Dad's over there." Eli shifts, pulling me into his lap.

"Did they get a ransom call? Is that why the FBI's involved?" Hope springs to life. If they want a ransom, maybe she's not dead, or worse.

"No. Dad called his supervisor and asked to be assigned to the case."

"He doesn't think it's the run-of-the-mill pedophile, does he?" Eli's dad is Special Agent John Malone. He works for the spook squad in the FBI. They are called in when there are paranormal elements involved.

"Dad's been tracking the case and there have been some new developments."

I finally look up. He's staring off into the distance, his eyes troubled.

"What kind of developments?" What new torture could Fate have drummed up for me now?

"He thinks it's a fallen angel, Deleriel, one of the first demons that fell with Lucifer. It rises once every one hundred and fifty years to feed off the souls of children."

"Why does he think that?" When did my life become a revolving episode of *Supernatural*?

"Do you remember that kid Mary's been babysitting for?" Eli strokes my hair absently, settling my nerves a bit. When I nod, he continues. "Seems the kid was supper for the demon. He'd been feeding from him. Mary fought it off, protected the kid, but there's a complication."

"Complication?" That doesn't sound at all good.

"We think it has a thing for Mary."

I sit straight up and lean back. "What?"

"It didn't hurt her. She said it gave her back the kid and then caressed her cheek. I think it wants her. Mary's soul is pretty pure. Something as black as that thing? She could feed it for centuries."

"It's not getting her." I mean that. Mary's been through too much to fall victim to a demon who'd do God knows what to her tortured soul. I won't let another person I love get hurt. Not if there's anything I can do to stop it.

"What's wrong with your eyes?" Eli cocks his head, studying my face. "Hilda?"

"Don't call me Hilda." I gently disentangle myself from Eli and stand. My eyes probably flashed black for a minute. They seem to do that when I get angry. I'm not getting into that with Eli yet. I don't know how he'll react.

The little old woman at the end of the hall waves to me. "Dear, can I speak with you?"

Then it hits me. She's a ghost. I'm so cold, I hadn't registered the temperature drop. It was only when Eli warmed me up that I noticed. She looks hesitant, almost afraid. I haven't been known to be the nicest person when it comes to ghosts, but then again, most of the ones I've dealt with wanted me dead.

Why not see what she wants? Maybe one good thing can come out of today. I walk down the hall toward her, and she smiles when I stop in front of her. "What can I do for you?"

"Mattie?" Eli is right behind me. "Who are you talking to?"

I ignore him and focus on the little grandma in front of me.

"I'm waiting for someone, my granddaughter. She's here in the hospital with her parents. Cancer. She's only three, but so beautiful." She's holding her knitting needles in her hand, and part of me tenses up, used to fighting off malignant ghosts. Eli can't see her, though, so it's a good sign. He can only see ghosts that have gone mad.

"I'm so sorry."

"All things happen for a reason, sweet girl." She reaches out and takes my hand. It's solid. Most ghosts can manage that if they try, but they can't maintain it for long. "You have to remember that."

"What do you mean?"

"I only have a moment. Things are coming, dark, dark things. You have to be prepared, little reaper, and remember that things always happen for a reason."

"I don't understand…"

She leans up and kisses my cheek then fades away.

What the heck was that about?

"Mattie who are you talking to?"

"A ghost." I turn and walk back down the hall. I need to check on Dan. All this talk of things happening for a reason pushes my panic button, and before I know it, I'm running. Caleb is standing at the nurses' desk speaking with one of the nurses. My face must have shown my alarm because he puts up a hand.

"He's fine. His CT is clear."

"Then what's making his nose bleed?" I demand, my panic level at high alert. What was that old woman talking about?

"It's not unusual for someone who's been on oxygen for days to have a minor nosebleed." Nurse Sunshine over there is way too peppy. My stare is enough to make her smile wilt.

"It wasn't minor. He soaked through an entire towel on the way here."

"She's right." I turn to see who I presume to be the doctor behind us. "The nose can bleed a lot. Most of the time, it's like a head wound. It looks worse than it is."

"But his head wound...he left too early."

"I agree he left too early." The doctor keeps her tone soothing. "I've checked his scan twice, and it's completely clear of any swelling or bleeding. I wanted to keep him overnight for observation, but he's having none of it."

"That sounds about like Officer Dan." Relieved, I let my panic recede a tiny bit. He's not dying. "He's more stubborn than I am."

"Not possible, Hilda."

I jab my elbow in Eli's ribcage, and he reacts like he's been delivered a killing blow. "Careful, there. You still owe me a proper date, and damaging the goods beforehand is not allowed."

"Mattie?"

The hint of a smile that had creased my face falls away when I see Jake's mom standing a few feet away. Flashes of Jake being shot by his brother flicker through my mind, of being chased, of watching Meg die. Seeing Mrs. Owens brings all those memories back, and I grip the edge of the nurses' station to keep from falling. My breathing speeds up and black spots start floating in front of my face.

The last thing I see is her face going from haggard to alarmed as I fall, the darkness eating away at my sight until there's nothing but blessed silence.

Chapter Nine

I rub a hand across my eyes, squinting at the bright sunlight. Did I faint? I'm not a fainter, but I'm pretty sure I fainted. The curtains blow, and I shiver at the bite to the breeze. When did it get cold? It's at least a hundred outside today. I stand, and two steps in, I trip and fall flat on my butt. What the...when did I put on heels? The black sequined shoes mock me from where they rest on my feet.

"What are you doing down there?" The British accent pulls my eyes up, and my gaze lands on aqua eyes. The man laughing down at me is tall, his hair as black as coal, and his skin dark, like he spends a lot of time out in the sun. He holds out his hand, and I take it. He pulls me up and plants a light kiss on my lips.

A baby's cry splits the air, and he laughs. "I'll go see to our son before the nanny can swoop in. You finish your toiletries."

When he lets go and strides out the door, all I can do is gape after him. Then I look down, another shock claiming me. I'm wearing a very short, sleek dress, the fringed ends telling me I'm in a flapper's dress from the early 1920's. My hand flies up to my head and I gasp. My long hair is gone, and instead it barely comes to my ears. Frantically, I look around for a mirror and find it in the corner. I stumble my way over to it and blink at what I see.

Dark honey gold hair is styled in a short wave as was the hairstyle back in that era. The dress is crimson, black lace trims the bodice, and the fringed beading is also black. A black choker with a cameo is around my neck. Blue eyes taunt me from a face I don't recognize.

Where the heck am I?

Another vision. It has to be another vision.

I lean down and take the heels off. I can't walk in the danged things.

"Going to Lisette's shoeless, are we? Now, that would be quite the fashion statement." I jump, startled at the sound of the unfamiliar voice. He's lounging in the doorway watching me. No, laughing at me.

I smile at his charming banter. I can't help it. This version of me loves this man. I can feel it in her bones.

"My feet hurt." I pick up the shoes and set them on the bed.

He pushes off the doorframe and glides over to me, a grin teasing his lips. "We can't have that, now, can we? Perhaps we should skip Lisette's party altogether. I'm sure we can find other things to do."

Ummm…no. Nope, nope, nope.

I slide away from him. "No, we should definitely go. She's expecting us. I'll put the shoes back on before we get there." Even the sound of my voice in its very posh English accent is weird.

"But I don't want to go."

I still at the sound of the gun being cocked.

Fudgepops.

I'm less than a foot away from the door. If I turn and look at him, it'll be too late. Instead of doing what he expects, I fall and roll out the door. The gun goes off, and I feel a sting in my side. I pay it no mind and get up, my feet flying down the stairs. The front door is locked, so I turn and run down a long hallway, checking each door as I go. The last one is open, and I hastily go in, closing it behind me.

A quick search for a weapon reveals nothing but books. I'm in a library. My first instinct is to hide under the desk, but instead I squeeze myself between two bookshelves. I'm barely small enough to fit.

He's coming. Footsteps echo down the hall, and the sound of each door being tried brings him closer and closer.

"Susan."

Fear pierces my heart, but along with it a deep sense of betrayal. I remember how this feels. I remember the pain, the confusion, the deep sense of grief at knowing the man I loved killed me. All those things are rushing back, filling me up.

The door creaks open, and he enters. His face is still its charming self; only his eyes have gone hard and cold. He's standing by the light mounted to the wall, its soft glow glinting blue highlights in his hair. The revolver is in one hand, and he's scanning the room. When he closes the door and walks into the room, I get a sinking feeling in the pit of my stomach. This isn't going to end well.

"I know you're in here, Susan. Please come out."

He's crazier than I think he is if he expects me to come out. The woman whose body I'm in is screaming inside, terrified of what's happening. So am I, but I'm smart enough to stay silent.

Just like I thought, he checks under the desk first and then frowns. He knows I'm in here. There were no other escape routes that I saw. But then maybe I wasn't supposed to find any other way out. Maybe all these dreams, or visions, or whatever are memories. What if I'm remembering what happened to me in past lives? Past lives with an aqua eyed man who murders me.

"Come out, my darling." The sound of his voice sends shivers through me. He sounds so sane, like a man who loves his wife.

He bends down and inspects something on the floor. He stands back up after a minute and starts walking. Straight toward me, his eyes downcast.

Blood drops. He's following a trail of blood drops from my wound. He'd shot me as I dived out of the bedroom. As soon as I realize what it is, my side begins to burn and ache like nobody's business. Why do you never feel the pain until you realize the wound is there? Why am I thinking about stupid stuff right now, anyway?

They lead him straight to the small alcove I've squeezed myself into. I know he can see me because I can see him. Those beautiful eyes I adore are so cold. He holds out his hand and simply waits. My body shakes, but I can't stop myself from taking his hand. He pulls me out, very gently. He leans his forehead against mine so all that I can see are his eyes.

"Why?" I whisper. "Why are you doing this?"

"Because I love you."

The sound of the shot echoes through the room and my knees buckle, the pain blooming in my stomach and then spreading outward. He pulls me into his arms as I bleed out, his eyes no longer cold, but soft and warm.

Those eyes are the last thing I see as my vision blurs then goes dark.

Chapter Ten

The sound of a whispered argument wakes me. I blink my eyes open to see people clustered a few feet away, their backs to me. My vision is a little blurry, but I'm pretty sure I know who it is.

"Dan?"

Before I can blink, he's right there. "You should have said you needed a nap."

A small bubble of laughter slips out. He's about the only person who can make me laugh when I'm scared out of my mind.

"Seriously, Mattie, are you okay?"

"Did I faint?"

"You went down like a pile of bricks." Eli moves into my field of vision, his hands stuffed into his pockets. Dan does that a lot when he's nervous or worried. Yet another trait the two of them share.

I shake my head. I fainted. I've been doing that a lot recently. I seriously need to get a handle on learning to deal with one shock right after the other.

I'm not expecting it when Eli squats in front of the chair I'm in. His eyes bring back the memory of the dream I'd just had, and my hands spread out over my abdomen. I can feel the bite of the bullet, and when I glance down, I fully expect to see the bloody wound, but it's not there.

"You just went white, Hilda. What's wrong?"

How to tell your maybe boyfriend you can't look at him right now? "I just need some space and you two are crowding me. Can you give me some breathing room?"

"Sure." Dan stands then puts out a hand for Eli to grab. Wait...what if Dan sees what I've been seeing? What if he sees the same murders I have? I start to shout a warning, but it's too late. Dan's eyes lose focus then roll back in his head.

Eli tries to pull his hand away, but he can't get Dan to let go.

"Hey, man, what gives?" Eli tries to pull away again, but it's useless.

"What's going on?" Mary and Caleb come over, both alarmed. "Dan? Hey, what's wrong? Mary, get a nurse!"

"No, wait." I stop him before he can call for the nurse. Mary is watching Dan, and I think she's caught on to what's happening. Caleb, on the other hand, is staring at me like I've lost my mind.

"Look at his eyes. He needs a doctor."

"No, Caleb, he doesn't." Mary places a hand on his arm. "He's seeing things."

"Dan woke up this morning with a new ability." My mouth sets in a grim line. He is not going to be happy about this, not if he is seeing what I've been reliving.

"New ability?"

"He can touch something or someone and get glimpses into their lives. We just found out about it earlier."

"He's psychic now?" Eli is still trying to pull his arm away from his brother. "Did it give him superhuman strength too?"

Then Dan lets go and stumbles away. He falls to his knees, heaving. "Don't touch him." I'm up and by his side faster than anyone else. "You okay?"

"Why didn't you tell me?" The accusation in his voice makes me wince. He saw it. Cat's out of the bag.

"Tell you what?" Eli asks, coming up behind us. "What did you see?"

"Eli, I wouldn't." I get up and block Eli from coming closer. "Getting near him right now is not a good idea."

"Why not?" The confusion in his voice is mirrored on Mary and Caleb's faces.

"Because he just saw you murder me twice. Well, maybe not me. I'm still not too sure about that."

"You're not making a bit of sense, Hilda." Frustration edges into his voice. "I haven't killed anyone. What are you talking about?"

"Do you remember when I told you about the dreams I was having? Of being someone else? The one where I got chased in the woods and stabbed to death, and then the one where I met your great something or other grandfather? I just had another one. I was in the 1920's, and I got shot. What I didn't tell anyone was the man who killed me in those dreams had your eyes, Eli. The same exact color eyes."

"That doesn't mean it's me." Horror and then panic settle in his expression. He understands what this means, even if he wants to deny it.

"We need to talk to Dad." Caleb's voice is quiet, but I can hear the undertone of fear in it.

"I didn't kill anyone, and I would *never* hurt Mattie."

"I don't think you'd do it intentionally." Dan stands and turns to face us. His eyes are haunted. "They loved the woman they murdered, Eli. They killed her because they loved her. Something is going on here. There's a reason she's having these dreams. A warning, maybe? I don't think you should be anywhere near her until we figure this out."

Eli opens his mouth to argue, but Caleb stops him. "Dan's right. We have to understand what those dreams mean.

Mom and Dad might be able to make sense out of all this."

"I think it has something to do with your ancestor." I rub my eyes. A headache is starting to bloom right behind my eyes. "In that dream, I wasn't afraid. No one tried to kill me. I think it all started with him."

"Then Mom will definitely know or at least be able to dig until she finds something. She's our historian." Caleb puts his hand on Eli's shoulder. "We'll figure this out."

My heart breaks a little when I see the defeat on Eli's face. I know it's probably the right thing to do, but I don't want to hurt him. It's why I kept that one detail to myself. I also know Dan and Caleb will keep Eli away from me, and I need him as much as I do Dan. "I'm sorry, Eli."

"Nothing to be sorry for, Hilda." He flashes me a smile. "We'll figure it out, and then you owe me that date."

"I'll call you when I get home. Promise."

"And Hilda? About the doc? Trust your instincts. If they say don't trust him, then don't let anyone pressure you into doing what you're not ready to do. Trust yourself." He gives me his cutest smile, dimples and all, then lets Caleb pull him away. We watch them disappear around the corner. With every step away from me he takes, I feel my heart crumple a little more.

"You should have told me."

He's so pissed. "Why? So you could've reacted like you are now? It's not Eli in those dreams. I didn't want you blaming him for something he didn't do."

"I'm gonna go find some coffee." Mary excuses herself, and I'm grateful. I hate having confrontations in front of people. Dan's not even paying attention. He's only focused on me.

"There's a reason you're seeing this stuff, Mattie. You didn't trust me enough to let me help you figure it out?"

I close my eyes against the hurt in his voice. "Of course I trust you, Dan. You're one of the few people I do, but you'd just met Eli. He turned your mom in to the cops. I didn't want to put one more nail in his coffin. You guys are just getting to know each other, to learn to be brothers. If I'd told you this? It might have derailed that for you."

"Mattie, you're more important to me than all of that."

"I didn't want to be the reason you hated your brother any more than you already did."

We both speak at the same time, then stop.

"You think I hate Eli?"

"Don't you?" I ask softly. "After everything he did, Dan. How can you not?"

"I don't hate him." He runs his hands through his hair then shoves them in his pockets. "I wanted to. I really, really wanted to, but I can't. I even understand what he did. He didn't know me or my family. All he saw was what this did to his family, and he reacted out of family loyalty. To Caleb and his dad. I would have turned her in myself after the shock had worn off. I can't hate him for doing what's right, Mattie."

"That's why I love you, Officer Dan. You always do what's right, even when it hurts." I wish I could be more like him sometimes.

"I love you too, Mathilda Louise Hathaway."

Something in his voice brings my eyes up to his. They are brimming with emotions I have no words for. They speak the words he can't say out loud. He loves me. I mean *love* loves me. A gasp falls through my lips at this realization. He loves me. The way I wanted him to. The knowledge curls up in my heart, pulling together all the broken, ragged ends of it. Plugging in the holes that have been open, bleeding wounds since I was five. He loves me.

"You should have told me, though." He looks away, and the moment is broken. "How can I protect you if I don't have all the facts? I'm a cop, Mattie. I need to see the evidence so I can understand how to solve the mystery."

"I can protect myself."

He laughs. "Yes, you can, better than most. But I'm in it for the long haul, Squirt. I am *always* going to be here to protect you, whether you want me to or not. So deal with it."

"I know." My voice cracks, and I clear my throat. I know Dan will be here for the long haul. He's proven it time and time again. He's my rock, and if I ever lost him, that'd be the end of Mattie Louise Hathaway. I don't think I could go on. "I'm sorry I didn't tell you."

"Yeah, well, just don't keep things from me again."

"I won't. I promise."

"Good." He nods and looks away. Is he crying? "You need to talk to Mrs. Owens if you're up for it. She's upset thinking she caused you to collapse."

"She did." I take his hint and change the subject. Neither of us is ready to discuss the things we need to, the things we can't talk about right now. "When I saw her, I had flashbacks from last night. Horrible, horrible flashbacks. I wasn't ready to see her, Dan."

"Then we can always come back in a few days." He walks over to me and pulls me into one of his patented Officer Dan bear hugs. Only this time, I know he loves me, and I feel so much more. I've always felt safe with Dan, safer than with anyone else, but now, I feel what its's like to be loved. Really and truly loved. For the first time in my life, I understand it.

"And Eli's right. I shouldn't have pushed you about Dr. Olivet. Your instincts are spot on. If you don't trust him, I can respect that."

"No, you were right too. I wouldn't have listened to him if he'd told me who he was. Maybe I did overreact a little. I don't trust him, Dan, but I can at least hear him out."

A laugh rumbles through him and into me. "As I live and breathe, I never thought I'd see the day when you'd admit you might be wrong about something."

"I'm not admitting anything. I'm just looking at different options."

"No, Squirt, you're growing up. Into a very capable, beautiful young woman who is going to be even more extraordinary than the girl you already are."

"Thank you."

"You ready to go home?" He pulls

away enough to look down at me.

Home? I start to say yes, and then remember my grandparents are about to show up. Nope, not ready to go home and face that. "No, let's go see Jake."

"You sure?"

"Yeah." Face your fears. That's always been my motto. I refuse to be scared anymore. I won't let the events of the last few months turn me into a victim.

Mattie Louise Hathaway…Crane is a survivor.

***

Mrs. Owens and her husband are talking in front of the nurses' station when Dan and I arrive on Jake's floor. I skid to a halt, the fear rushing back. Just seeing her makes me start to have flashbacks. Only this time I'm prepared, and it doesn't overwhelm me. Dan's hand on my back steadies me. His gentle whispers in my ear quiets the panic and helps it to recede. Eli can calm me down instantly, but Dan does it in a different, more natural way. It's his presence. It inspires safety and trust.

Mr. and Mrs. Owens approach us cautiously. God only knows what my face must look like if her own is etched in sorrow. She's aged a good ten years since the last time I saw her. The last twenty-four hours has been harder on her than me. I survived, but her sons didn't. One is dead, and the other fighting for his life. It's not fair. Not at all. She's good people and doesn't deserve this.

"Mattie. I am so sorry."

I press myself into Dan, taking a moment to gain a little courage. "You don't have anything to be sorry for. None of this is your fault."

"But it is." Her voice breaks and she pulls in a deep breath, her eyes brimming with tears. "I keep thinking to myself what I did, what could I have done to prevent this? He was my son. I must have done something wrong for him…"

"No, Mrs. Owens. Please don't blame yourself. I don't, and I know Jake doesn't. He thinks you're the best mom in the world, and I agree. If I had a mom,

I'd want her to be like you."

A tear leaks out of her eyes, and her husband squeezes her hand, giving me a thankful smile. He must have been worried I'd blame her for all of this too. I can't even imagine what they've been going through. To realize the son you loved and raised to be a good person turns out to be a psychopath has to be unsettling. Then having said son shoot the other one? They must be going through a nightmare right now.

"How's Jake?" Dan shifts closer, putting his arm around me.

"He's not so good." Mr. Owens turns his head, looking through an open door. I follow his gaze, but can't see anything except a closet and what's probably the door to the bathroom. "They asked us a few minutes ago if we want to consider pulling him off life support. They don't think he's going to get better."

"I'm sorry." Dan's arms tighten around me as he speaks. "No one should have to make that decision."

"We don't want him to suffer." Mr. Owens wipes a tear away. "I think he's been through enough already. It's the right thing to do."

Hearing him try to justify his actions to himself sends shards of pain through my heart. He loves Jake so much. His dad was his world too. I remember sitting on their couch listening to the two of them tell me stories about all the crazy things they did together.

"Can I say goodbye to him?" Jake saved my life. I owe him a goodbye.

"Of course." Mrs. Owens can't quite bring herself to smile. "We were hoping you'd come by before we let them...before..." She can't finish the sentence. A sob rips through her, and her husband pulls her close, his own shoulders shaking from the sobs he can't hold in.

I wipe my own tears away with the back of my hand. This is awful. Jake and his family don't deserve any of this. They're good people. Dan pushes me past them, and we go into Jake's room.

He's lying there, hooked up to every tube known to man. The steady beeping of the machines disturbs the utter quiet.

The blinds are closed, the lights down. A death watch. That's what this room reminds me of. When people are ready to die, they shroud the room in darkness. He looks so helpless lying there. So unlike the vibrant guy I knew. Looking at him like this doesn't bring back memories of the nightmare I'd lived through, only memories of the boy who'd been my friend.

Without him, Meg and I would never have managed to get away. He saved us. I break away from Dan and open the blinds. I turn on the lights. He doesn't deserve this. He deserves to be in the light. He is a good person. He reminds me of Dan, really. He worked to help his parents pay the bills and put food on the table. He's a decent guy.

Dan leans against the wall, watchful, ready to help when I need him.

Pulling the chair up beside the bed, I sit down. I was pretty sure he'd already been reaped last night, but maybe I was wrong. His hand is ice cold when I take it in mine, and I know in that moment I wasn't wrong. Jake's gone. This is just an empty shell with no soul. He's gone.

"I'm so sorry," I whisper, letting my tears fall. "I'm so sorry this happened to you, Jake. I wanted to thank you too. You saved me last night, and I am so sorry there's nothing I can do to help you."

"Mattie, I don't think there's anything you could do even if you wanted to." Dan moves closer, his voice soft and soothing. "Jake wouldn't want you to feel guilty. I knew him. He was a good kid."

"He's not here." I clutch his hand tighter. "His soul is already gone."

"You're sure?"

I nod woodenly. It's one of the few things I am sure of. He's not in any pain. He's gone to a better place where there will never be any more pain. Only joy and happiness. Football Sunday every day.

I wish I could tell his parents it's okay to pull the plug, that he's not with us anymore. It might ease their pain, but I'd just sound crazy or like I was trying to assuage their guilt at letting him go.

This isn't fair. I think about his parents, about the pain they are going through. It's going to kill them. Losing them both will kill them. To lose them both. It's so cruel.

I'm religious, very religious, but at times like this, even I have to wonder why God does what He does. Our role is not to question, but to accept, but sometimes that's hard. Especially right now. It's hard to accept without question the pain the Owens family is going through.

It's hard to accept everything happens for a reason…

Happens for a reason.

The little grandma's words come back to me. She told me to accept it. But what reason could this have happened for? His soul is gone, but his body is alive…

No.

Could I?

What would happen if I did, though? Would that freaky angel come down and smite me? I'd upset the balance of the living and the dead…but why else was his body left here when his soul is gone?

I don't even know if I can do it.

Well, no harm in trying, and if the

powers that be get mad, they get mad. I close my eyes and start looking inside myself for that ball of bright blue light that is my reaping ability. It only takes me a moment to find it. Inside that light resides a soul, a soul I'd reaped. He'd sacrificed himself to save me. What if I could give him back his life? Give the Owens back their son, or at least someone to love?

Why else would that little granny have said those words to me if I'm not supposed to remember them? To apply them?

Part of me is crying out to stop, that it's not right. The reaper in me says it's not right, but every other part of me that is human is screaming to do it. That we can at least right one wrong, we can gain something good out of this tragedy.

I don't think about it anymore. Instead I remember my Mirror Boy. I remember his laughter, his pain. I remember the first time he kissed me. I remember the way he protected me from everyone. How he stayed with me while I lay dying, how he refused to leave me. I remember

how he sacrificed his light so I could live.
I remember him.

His soul rises out of the blue light,
unsure and unsteady. I reach out and
wrap my own light around it, making him
feel safe and loved. Then I pull him
toward the body on the bed, the empty
shell waiting for new life.

Dan gasps behind me, but I keep my
attention on the soul in my hands. I coax
him, make him understand what I am
giving him. I am giving him life. I am
giving him a way back. I am giving him
all the love I have inside to give him. I
watch as the glowing ball of white light
that is my Mirror Boy glides toward Jake
and hovers there for a moment, hesitant.
Then it settles into Jake, and I crumple
onto the chair, feeling like I've just run a
one-hundred-mile marathon.

"What did you just do, Mattie?" Dan's
voice is awed, frightened. "You were
glowing. This blue light sort of lit up all
around you."

Come on, wake up. Please wake up.

One of the monitors begins to beep. It
had been silent before. I recognize it. It's

the one they'd used to monitor Dan's brain activity in the hospital. It's coming to life. A smile spreads across my face until I see him.

The reaper who'd come to collect Dan is standing at the foot of the bed. He's still wearing the same jeans and t-shirt I remember, but he's not frowning.

"I wondered if you'd put two and two together before it was too late."

They're not mad?

He smiles. "Sometimes lives are cut short, and they weren't able to do what they are meant to do. Everything *does* happen for a reason."

Then he's gone. My breath comes out in a hard sigh. Laughter escapes me as I stare at all the monitors around us coming to life.

"Wake up." The words are ripped out of me, hope flaring to life. "Listen to the sound of my voice. Wake up."

His eyes flutter, their lids moving frantically, and then he opens them.

The bluest eyes I have ever seen blink at me.

He's awake.

Chapter Eleven

Amidst all the doctors and the nurses, only one thing shines through. He's awake. The Owens are ecstatic. A medical miracle, the doctors are calling it. Brain dead. Now he's awake and breathing on his own. Granted, he *was* shot, so he's in a lot of pain. That's not something shoving a soul into an empty body can fix.

Dan hasn't said a word to me. He keeps looking at me with this strange expression I can't quite place. He knows I did something, but not what.

"I'm gonna go find something to drink in the cafeteria. Do you want something?"

He shakes his head. And just like that,

we're back to the silent treatment. I know he has issues with all this supernatural stuff, but you'd think for a man who can see enraged ghosts, met a reaper *and* an angel, and is now a little psychic, he'd be more adept at handling this type of thing.

"Come get me when we can go in?"

Again with the nod. He's more freaked out than I'd thought. I guess the glowy me will take him a few minutes to process.

When I pass by Jake's room, there are still a horde of doctors and nurses in there. I see the Owens pacing a few feet down the hall. They stop when they see me, and even though I dread this conversation, I can't keep the grin off my face when Mrs. Owens hugs me.

"I don't know what you did, Mattie, but you brought our boy back." There are tears in Mr. Owens eyes. "Thank you."

"I didn't do anything, Mr. Owens…"

"No." Mrs. Owens shakes her head, and her eyes burn with an intensity that makes me believe she knows exactly what I did. Maybe she does. She was always the most religious person I know.

Maybe God did answer her prayers by sending me in that room. "We've been praying since the police showed up at our house. There was no hope. We knew it. I'm not going to demand answers from you, Mattie. Just know we are grateful."

"I'm glad he's awake," I murmur and disentangle myself. "I'm going to get something to drink. Can I bring you guys back something?"

Before they can answer, one of the nurses pokes her head out the door and calls them into Jake's room. I smile as they all but run down the few feet to their son's room. At least one good thing came out of this nightmare.

The elevators are slow, so I smash the down arrow repeatedly. I know it doesn't make it go any faster, but it helps me. When it finally dings and opens, I step aside as people file out. Once inside, I hit the first floor button and close my eyes to wait for the short ride to end. It's quiet and soothing in the elevator, and for the first time all day, I let out the deep breath I've been holding.

I survived.

Relief. I should be embarrassed and ashamed to feel relief, but I'm not. Maybe that makes me the selfish person everyone thinks I am, but I survived. I survived.

And I managed to save a person in the process. Eric will get the chance to live his life, and Jake's parents won't have lost everything. It's a good day.

At least that's what I tell myself when the elevator doors open and interrupt my mental bolstering. I step out and automatically turn left. I know the layout of Carolinas Medical Center better than most. I've been here enough to know where everything is.

Only I'm not in the hallway leading to the cafeteria. It's dim, and I hear the clanking of pipes. Where the heck am I? The sound of the elevator doors closing makes me turn and look. There's a big letter B lit up. I'm in the basement? How did I end up in the basement?

I press the up button and nothing happens—no lights, no whirring of the elevator. Nada. I see the stairwell door and try that, but it doesn't budge. I pound on the elevator button again, and still nothing. Great, just freaking great. I'm stranded in the basement with no phone.

Letting out a sigh, I turn around. It stinks down here. That's the first thing I notice. It's like they'd dumped all the old garbage and rotting food in one place and the stench took over. Funky garbage is a smell I'm going to forever remember.

The second thing I see is the sign on the wall I'd missed before. We're in the basement, and there's only one thing they keep in the basement—the morgue.

The old lights overhead flicker and cast shadows over the walls. Cold too. Freezing, really. I search the empty hallway, the first warning bells going off in my head.

Something's down here with me.

Keeping my back against the wall, I inch away from the elevator door. The clank of the water pipes startles me. The white tile floor is dingy, stained. The green walls might have once been bright, but they haven't been painted in Lord knows how many years. They're discolored with what I don't even want to know.

A whoosh of air curls through the ducts, and I jump. The AC. It's just the AC kicking on. *Deep breath, Mattie. Stay calm.*

A few months ago, I might have believed all I had to do was close my eyes and ignore them, but I know better now. Ghosts have the ability to physically hurt you. I've experienced it firsthand.

A little girl's laughter floats down the hallway. I can't tell if it came from the left or the right. It seems to fill up the space. The sound of running footsteps go right past me and straight toward the morgue.

I am not going into the morgue. Nope, not happening. Nothing is going to make me go into the morgue.

Except maybe the shuffling coming straight at me.

I squeeze my eyes shut. God knows what type of horrific traffic victim is roaming the halls. Hospitals are flooded with ghosts. It's why I hate going anywhere near them. They haven't bothered me so much the last few times I was admitted. Why, I don't know, but that's changed. I saw them all last night and again today when I came in. Crowding around me, demanding help.

But down here? In the dark with no one around? The regular ghosts don't congregate down here. Only the darkest ones roam the shadows. The ones that terrify the other ghosts.

The stench of decay and rot surrounds me.

I know you can see me.

The words are hoarse and drawn out, like it's speaking through a long tunnel. It's right beside me, its foul breath skating over my cheek as it whispers in my ear. The cold seeps into my bones, the ache enough to make me wince.

My body quivers when it pushes in closer, its hot rancid breath all that I can inhale. I turn my face away, trying to escape the smell, but it invades my space. I squirm a few more inches away from it so I can take a few shallow breaths.

Look at me.

But I don't want to.

I can feel its anger, though. If I don't look, it might do me some serious damage. I crack open my left eye and peer sideways.

Disgust. Horror. Fear.

I'm not sure which emotion to feel once I get a good look at the ghost. Its face isn't really a face anymore. It's mostly a skull, with chunks of flesh still sticking onto the bones. Only one eye remains, the green orb staring lazily at me. What little skin and tissue is left on its face is rotting, the pus oozing out. It drips to the floor, splattering my shoes. More of it falls, the wet, sticky substance making this awful splat sound.

It's like its flesh is melting, the tissues giving in to infection and falling away, the blackish diseased mixture dripping down the bones.

Then it smiles at me.

Fear overrides every other emotion. "What…what do you want?"

You.

That's it. I hit the hallway at a dead run, not caring the only place I can run to is the morgue. It's moving behind me. I can hear the sluggish footsteps coming down the hall. It's not running. Nope, it's pulling the Michael Myers trick of walking, which only makes me run faster. I've seen way too many horror movies.

The doors leading to the morgue are ahead of me. I hit them and push on the metal bar to let me in. It opens with no resistance, and I slam it behind me. I gulp air into my lungs. I need a second to catch my breath.

My eyes flicker over the room, and I can't stop the relief from bubbling up. I'm not in the actual morgue. I'm in the front room. There's a desk with an abandoned half-eaten sandwich and bottle of Mountain Dew sitting on it. Another set of double doors is to the left of the desk. File cabinets line the opposite wall.

The godawful scent of rot tickles my nose. It's right behind me, outside the door. There's only one other place to go. The morgue autopsy room.

Frustrated, I make a beeline for the other room. I'm not letting that thing touch me again. I feel…a shudder rolls over me. I need a shower. That's what I feel like. Unclean and in need of a shower.

This room is exactly as I imaged. One wall contains at least a dozen of those small cubby-like freezers. Lab equipment lines the opposite wall. Two doors are on the wall right in front of me. Offices, maybe.

In the middle of the room are three large stainless steel tables, various surgical instruments, and a standing scale beside them. All but one are unoccupied. A small form is draped on the center table. The kid I heard earlier. It has to be her.

A quick search of the room reveals nothing. It's freezing in here, which tells me the kid's here somewhere.

"Little girl?"

A squeaking noise catches my attention, and I turn my head to see the sink in the middle of the lab equipment turn on. Not a lot, just enough to let a few drops start to drip. Frost begins to creep outward from the sink, covering the stainless steel and crawling down the counter like a vine twisting its way toward me. The walls, cold and sterile to begin with, crust over with ice crystals, and the ice spreads downward to the white tile floor. It flows toward the center of the room, toward the one metal table and the tiny body.

My back presses against the doorway, not caring if the rotting thing outside gets in or not. I can't take my eyes off the table and its draped occupant. The ice reaches the table legs and twines upward at a dizzying speed.

I stare, frozen, at the sheet.

It rises and falls, like someone breathing. Crap on toast. This isn't good. Not at all.

The body beneath the sheet sits up, the sheet sticking to it. It looks like someone under a sheet, pretending to be a ghost. I know better. I know what's under there. Its head turns in my direction, and I stop breathing altogether.

Malevolent. What's under there is no longer the ghost of a child. It's full of hate and rage. Evil. That's what's under the sheet—evil.

I think I'm gonna take my chances with Mr. Stinky outside. I push backwards, but the door refuses to give. I slam my entire backside into it, and still it won't budge.

Fudgepops.

A small hand slips into mine.

I let out a shriek and try to pull my hand away, but she holds on. The child who's clutching my hand like a lifeline is about six or seven. Curly blonde hair is streaked through with matted red, brown, and black stains. There's a large gash right above the worst of the stains. Other than that, there's not a mark on her. Her brown eyes bulge with the same fear that has paralyzed me.

I'm scared.

"Me too, kid."

It's hungry.

What? Hungry…a flashback from my dream last night invades my memory. Those things had devoured that kid. I glance down at the child beside me. She's so terrified she's shaking.

"I promise it's not going to get you."

Tears well up in her eyes, and she

whimpers.

"You shouldn't make promises you can't keep."

My head snaps up, and I see a figure standing beside the table. He's wearing a cloak, the hood hiding his face. His voice sends tiny icicles through my veins, threatening to tear them open. The pain makes me gasp, but I pull the little girl closer. Whatever that thing is, it's not getting her.

The sheet starts to fall, and it's like a train wreck. I can't look away as the sheet drops and reveals his face, his shoulders. I know this kid. I've seen him on the news. He was taken from one of the parks downtown. The last victim in a string of missing children whose bodies were later found. He's African American, his black hair buzzed short. Long, bloody gashes have all but shredded his arms. His bottom lip is torn, the flap of skin bouncing gently against his chin, exposing his teeth. It's hard to see the bruising on his face because it's so dark, but I can make out the discoloration.

His eyes, though. They pull a scream

from the little girl desperately holding onto me. Those eyes are empty, cold. The color is a bright yellow, with a few streaks of red and green enhancing the jewel-like hue. I've seen eyes similar to these. Last night in my dream. Only the dream boy had clear, yellow eyes. Not a hint of another color in them.

Those hungry eyes bore into me. A wave of dark hatred rolls off the thing sitting on the cold metal table and crashes into me.

I push frantically against the door, but it's stuck. Whatever these things are, they're keeping me here. I can't escape. They're not demons. They're not shades. They're not even ghosts. They can mimic a ghost. What are they?

Please, please, help me.

The little girl is tugging on my hand, begging me to save her. The thing that used to be a child slides off the table, its yellow eyes glued to us. Hunger pulsates in them. The cloaked figure glides around the table, facing us.

"You can see them."

He sounds so shocked. Definitely not a

ghost. Ghosts always know I can see them.

"Why can you see us?" He moves closer, and I flinch, the girl sobbing into my leg. He sniffs, much like a dog who's trying to determine if something is friend, foe, or food.

"A living reaper." He sounds pleased this time, like he's discovered lost treasure. Happy. Why is he happy?

The creature standing beside him crouches, preparing to launch. The little girl folds herself into me, terrified. It's going to get her. I know it instinctively. This child who has placed her trust in me, ghost or not, is going to be consumed.

What can I do? I could try to do what I did in New Orleans with the deranged ghost, but that uses energy and these things feed off ghost energy. Anything I try to do with my reaping abilities will only give them what they want.

What else?

The Between. I can open the Between. That space between the planes, the space reapers guide souls through on their journey into the next plane of existence.

There are things there, scary creatures that might even make these two look like puppies, but I can't let them get this innocent child. Her soul shines like a brilliant white light, blinding in its intensity, and they're hungry.

It's so easy, I don't even have to think about it. Once I decide to do it, it's like the part of me that is a reaper takes over, and the doorway opens. It looks like one of those TV channels with no picture. All snowy and staticky. White noise. It could almost be soothing if you can get past the cries of the monsters lurking within.

"We have to go." I clutch her hand. She'll be okay as long as I can keep hold of her.

The cloaked figure watches silently, freaking me out even more. The monster at its feet opens its mouth, a horrifying moan echoing, erupting.

I waste not another moment. "Hold tight."

Then we jump.

Chapter Twelve

White. Everywhere. No walls, no ceiling, no floor, no landscape…just endless white expanse. The cold is so intense it burns away every lucid thought, every feeling, every sensation. Nothing but the bitter iciness of winter. My body is numb, the sheer shock of the cold freezing me in place. I've never been in here. I've fallen through it before, but for never more than a few seconds.

The little girl is shaking. I feel her hugged up against me. She's as cold as I am. At least that thing didn't get to eat her. A howl breaks through the silence and we both go still, listening. Several growls sound all around us. We might still be on the dinner menu.

I don't see anything, but I know they're here. Is it because I'm not a full reaper that I can't see the monsters that inhabit the Between? Did I save us from one beast only to lead us into the waiting maw of another?

Where are we?

"We're in the Between." I put my arm around her. "It's the place between the different planes."

Are there monsters here?

"Yes." My eyes scan the expanse again, but it remains empty.

Can we go now?

If only I knew how to get out of here, we'd have been gone, like, yesterday.

"What are you doing here?"

I know that voice. I look behind me, and sure enough it's the reaper who'd told me I could put Eric's soul in Jake's body. His glare is hot enough to light a fire under the devil himself.

"Hiding?"

"Hiding? In the Between? Are you crazy?"

"Uh, no, but we were desperate, and it was the only way I could find to get out and keep this little girl safe."

His eyes swoop down and the hardness in his face eases. It becomes softer, his expression morphing to concern and compassion. "Hello, Hailey."

"How do you know her name?"

"Reapers always know the names of the souls we look for."

Huh. Well, I had no clue what her name was.

"What were you hiding from?"

Monsters. They wanted to eat us.

"Eat you?"

I explain to him about the two things we encountered in the morgue, and his expression tightens, the fear in his eyes unmistakable.

"What? What were they?"

"Deleriel has risen."

"That fallen angel thingy Eli was telling me about?"

"Take my hand, Mattie. I need to get the two of you out of here before the wraiths surround us."

"I don't see anything."

"Take my hand." I lay my hand in his, and the entire landscape morphs so fast, my head gets dizzy. We are in a forest, the shadows deep and dark. No moon sheds light into the thick trees, but I can see, nonetheless. I can also see the creatures lurking behind the trees, moving like cheetahs, their cries louder, more intense. Black shadows. I think I preferred blind bliss to seeing what wants to eat me.

"Holy crap."

"Exactly." The reaper squeezes my hand, and I pick Hailey up. She's not going to be able to keep up with us on her own.

"Your instincts are getting better." He tugs on my hand and we start walking.

We're not running for our lives? Does he really want us to take a nice leisurely walk through the woods, with all the monsters gnashing their teeth at us?

"Shouldn't we put a little scoot in our boot?" Even I can hear the tremors of fear in my voice. Now that I can see the big bads, I want as far away from them as I can get.

He stops and turns to stare at me, his expression incredulous. "Scoot in my boot?"

"It means to hurry up." I glance around and hold onto Hailey tighter. "I don't think walking is going to save us."

"That's part of the problem, Mattie. You're always in a hurry. If you'd stop and take a few minutes to think, you wouldn't get yourself in trouble so much."

Seriously, reaper boy is trying to lecture me? "I don't care what you think about me, but I didn't save this kid from being eaten just to let these creatures do the same thing."

He cracks a smile. "I may have misjudged you."

"Can we run and talk at the same time?" The guy needs to get a move on. I swear, if these things come at us, he's the first to go. I will drop kick him and run for my life.

"They can't touch you as long as you hold my hand." He gives Hailey a reassuring smile, only she can't see it since her face is buried in my neck. She's still crying, poor kid.

"And why is that?"

"Because I'm protected from them. That protection extends to whomever I'm escorting. It's the souls that break away, that wander off or wind up here by accident that are consumed."

"So it's a reaper thing?"

"Yes, it's a reaper thing." He nods before continuing. "You are only a half-reaper right now. Your gifts are new, just waking up. Over time, you'll begin to see the Between the way we do and navigate it safely."

"Over time?" So my ghost skills are going to get a power up? Awesome. All the better to protect myself.

"You are a special case, Mattie Hathaway. Most living reapers never discover their abilities. One has to die in order to awaken those gifts. Even then, the most they can do is see the souls searching for a way off this plane. They can talk with them, get them to look for the light. There's never been a living reaper who could open the doorway to the Between, let alone see into the light and fight off a full-fledged reaper."

I shrug. "I got skills."

"Yes, you do. A unique set of skills we need, especially now."

What's he going on about?

"Have you been made aware of your genealogy yet?"

My genealogy?

"Your mother's family." He pauses, his face screwed up as if he's trying to come to some kind of epic decision.

"You mean about them breeding with demons?" It's not something I want to chat about just now, surrounded by a small horde of hungry wraiths.

"Yes." He looks away from me, his face morphing to one of stern determination. "We try not to interfere, to let things run their ordinary course, but there is nothing ordinary about you. You need to understand the role you play. This is the only place we can talk about this. No one can hear us here."

Crap on toast, this doesn't sound at all good.

"You are part demon, part reaper, and something else. Something that's hidden even from me. That is the part that scares the head honchos upstairs. You're unpredictable. You're loyal. What you did to save Dan…what he did to stay with you? That scares them, Mattie, but they need you. It's why you're still alive. They need you."

I am part demon? Holy fudgepops. I want to throw up.

"Focus, Mattie! We don't have much time. You're a perfect storm, the perfect trifecta. Part demon, part reaper, part something undefinable. Figure out what that last part is, and you'll be able to protect yourself from all of them."

"Wait, protect myself from everyone?"

"Mattie, the moment you defeat Deleriel, they'll eliminate you."

Eliminate me? What the…? "Wait just a minute, buster!"

"There's no more time." He glances to the right, and I see the pathway winding to a doorway. It's the doorway I can sometimes see in the light. The one with two paths, dark and light. He takes Hailey from me. "I will take her from here. Remember what I said. Be safe, Mattie Louise Hathaway."

When I blink, I'm back in the elevator.

It dings and the doors open. I'm back on the third floor. Jake's floor. I stumble forward, getting out of the elevator as fast as I can. I'm dying of thirst, but no way am I getting anywhere near that elevator alone.

Dan's still sitting where I left him. When he sees me, he gives me a little wave. "I thought you were thirsty?"

"You over your shock yet?"

"So I had a freak out moment. Sue me."

"I just had an epic freak out moment, so keep your virtual millions."

He quirks an eyebrow in question, and I tell him about my morgue adventure and then my chit chat with Reaper Boy. He listens, never interrupting me. When I'm done, he sits back and rubs his chin thoughtfully.

"So you're telling me not only do we have to worry about demons, but angels want you dead too?" He laughs.

He laughs? I'm panicking, and he's laughing? "What gives? This is not funny, Officer Dan."

"Yeah, it kinda is." He doubles over,

he's laughing so hard. "Only you could piss off Heaven and Hell."

"Do I look like I find this funny at all?"

"Mattie?"

Dan's laughter dries up as soon as we see Mrs. Owens standing in the doorway leading to Jake's room.

"He's awake if you'd like to see him."

I scramble off the chair I'd collapsed in and move swiftly toward Mrs. Owens, only half listening to her. He's awake.

He's not sitting up and talking. I didn't expect that. I mean, he was shot, after all. The physical body needs to heal.

"Jake, honey, Mattie's here to see you. Do you remember her?"

He turns his head and looks at me, his eyes so blue they could make the clearest sky weep from envy. He blinks them several times. "I know you."

"Of course you know me."

"He's having some memory problems." Mr. Owens shuffles around the bed, cutting off my view of him. "He doesn't know who he is, who we are. It's a blank slate. And his eyes…"

"His eyes?"

Mrs. Owens takes a shuddering breath. "Jake's eyes have always been brown, but now they're blue."

Oh no. Why are his eyes blue? The soul isn't supposed to make physical changes. At least I don't think so.

"I don't care." Mrs. Owens voice is soft, calm, even. "I have my son back. His eyes could be purple and his skin blue and I wouldn't care."

Mr. Owens places a hand on my shoulder. "We don't care. Even if he has to learn to love us all over again, we don't care."

"All over again?"

"The doctors say he may never regain his memory. They don't know everything about the brain, but they do know he was clinically brain dead. His memory, everything that made him Jake, it could all be gone."

"I'm so sorry." Had I been wrong to do this? It's just like taking Jake from them all over again.

"Don't be, Mattie. He's our son. We love him no matter what. We always will.

He'll get to know us again, to love us, to understand how much we love him."

"Can I have a few minutes alone with him?" I need to see what's going on with him. I can only pray Eric remembers who he is. His soul is confused right now. I'm not surprised he's having issues adapting and that his memory is scrambled.

"Of course. I think we'll go find some coffee." Mr. Owens places his hand on the small of his wife's back and leads her out the door, leaving me alone with Jake…Eric. I'm not sure what to call him.

I go further into the room, and my heart breaks at the confused frustration on his face. "Hello."

"I know you." Even his voice is beyond frustrated.

"Yes, you do. I'm Mattie."

"Mattie." He says the word, trying it out.

"Do you remember your name?"

"They told me it was Jake." He scrunches up his nose, and I know the name doesn't sit well with him. "I don't know…I just can't remember anything."

I sit on the edge of his bed and take his hand in mine. "I know it's scary. You feel all alone, but you're not. You have me and your parents. I promise you're not alone."

He's staring at his hand in mine, his eyes a little unfocused. "I know that I know you, Mattie Hathaway. I know it."

He said my last name. He remembers me. Maybe. He could be accessing the part of Jake's brain where his memories were. Do your memories leave with your soul, or does your brain work like one big hard drive, storing things in different files and folders?

I have no clue what I'm doing here. I should have asked Reaper Boy before he kicked me out of the Between. Only he was too busy giving death warnings.

"You look upset."

"No." I do my best to keep my tone reassuring. "I'm not upset. You have no idea how happy I am to see you awake."

"I don't think my name is Jake." He searches my eyes, looking for any hint that he's right. I don't know what to tell him. Could filling in the blanks do more harm than good right now?

"Why don't you get some rest? I think that'll help you get your memories back faster than anything else. Besides, it's not every day you survive a gunshot wound and a head injury. Get some sleep, Jake. We'll be here for you when you wake up. Promise."

He nods, his eyes already drooping, and I stand and cut his overhead light off.

There is one person I can talk to about all this who might know what to do.

But am I willing to talk to him?

For Eric? Yeah, I am.

Chapter Thirteen

Dan's sitting in the passenger seat looking disgusted. He's not Super Man. He has limits. The man almost died from a head wound, and he's not well. If it were up to me, he'd be right there in the hospital next to Eric. Even the doctors advised him to stay overnight and let them monitor him, but he refused. I didn't learn that little tidbit of information until we were in the car, getting ready to leave. So I pitched a fit and made him let me drive.

"What do you know about the missing kids case?" I need to learn as much as I can. If Deleriel is taking them and they seem to keep finding me, I'm pretty sure I'll have to stop him in order to keep those creepy little yellowed eyed monsters away from me.

"They're not missing anymore, Mattie."

"I know, but it's easier to say that instead of saying all the murdered kids, okay? What's happening to them is awful."

"I know." He lets out a heavy sigh and turns to face me. "Zeke and I were talking last night. We think the ghost that attacked you at his place was one of them. Whatever is happening to them is beyond awful. They're being tortured in ways I can't even imagine."

I still don't remember that. Yet another thing to discuss with the Spook Doctor.

"What else do you know? Were you even there when they started to disappear?"

He nods. "For the first couple, yeah. It wasn't my case, though, so I only know the basics."

"Can you get a hold of the files?" I know it's a lot to ask, especially since he's in trouble over looking into the deaths of the girls whose ghosts tried to kill me a few days ago. I don't think his captain has had time to chew him out yet.

"Probably." He fiddles with the radio, finally settling on Kiss 95.1 and turns it down to barely a whisper. My favorite station. Dan has no real favorites. He just listens to whatever station is playing music he likes. "Brody is in charge of the investigation."

"Awesome. He loves me."

"Yeah, but it's not you who has to ask him to see the files, now, is it?"

True.

"I'll figure something out." He rubs his head, his eyes closing.

"Headache?"

"Yeah. It's gotten worse since I picked up that toy. I honestly thought it was a brain bleed or something causing the visions. I *hoped* it was."

"Is it every time you touch something or just some of the time?"

"I've touched stuff since I woke up and I've only had two visions. Once with that toy and once with Eli. It's kind of random."

Or is it? "Dan, do you think you'd be

willing to try to use your vision to help Kayla?"

"What do you mean?"

"I mean maybe pick up the teddy bear we found this morning, and…"

"No."

"I know all this supernatural stuff isn't what you wanted, Dan, but if we could…"

"You don't understand, Mattie. What if I pick it up and I see what they did to her, are doing to her?" His voice is haunted, bleak. "I don't think I can handle that."

Sometimes I forget he's not used to seeing the violence I am. Ghosts in all their mutilated glory have been haunting me since I was five. Dan? A couple weeks at best. Plus, I know there's nothing I can do to help the ghost who seeks me out. With Dan's ability, he could very well see someone torturing Kayla, and he'd be helpless to do anything but watch. He's a cop. His first instinct is to protect. It would haunt him forever, but there is something he'd never be able to forgive himself for.

"But what if you could actually save

her?" I ask softly. "Could you live with yourself knowing you might have done something to prevent her death?"

After that, the car ride goes silent. Even the gentle hum of the radio seems hushed. I know asking him to do this is horrible, but I know that little girl. I talk to her. Sometimes when no one else is around, I've even played hopscotch with her. She's a good kid, and if there's something I can do to bring her home, I will. Even if that means asking Dan to do something he's not comfortable with.

When Dan finally speaks, his voice is calm, but so quiet it's almost a whisper. "Drive to the station."

Chapter Fourteen

Dan

CMPD is a war zone when we finally get there. A missing kid will do that, especially one who might be the next victim of our serial killer. Mattie tensed up the moment we entered the building. She's got a rap sheet half a mile long, though. Most of the cops know her too. She's rubbed them all wrong at one time or another when she got hauled in. To be fair, since I've met her, she hasn't been brought in for anything other than to answer questions about her mother.

Well, there was that incident of breaking and entering she roped me into helping with, but she managed to sweet talk our way out of that one.

I shake my head ruefully. She suckered me into committing a crime to help out a cat that turned out to be a boa constrictor. The things that girl has gotten me into over the last year.

"Richards!"

I wince at the sound of my captain's shrill bark. She still hasn't been able to ream me out over the last case I stuck my nose into. Granted, we did manage to solve a set of murders that spanned several counties. So, hopefully, she'll take that into consideration.

I switch course and head to her office instead of checking in with a couple guys I know who'll give me the four-one-one on the case.

"What are you doing here, Richards?" She wastes no time getting right to the point. Her abruptness and ability to cut to the chase fast tracked her to the position of captain.

"I wanted to check on the investigation, see if there are any leads."

She eyeballs Mattie behind me and then goes into her office. "Both of you get in here and close the door."

Mattie is wide-eyed and her shoulders are ramrod straight when she marches into the room ahead of me. I can only hope she keeps her mouth shut. Captain Warner won't put up with it for a second.

"Sit down."

The frown on my girl's face is shouting that she's about to say something she shouldn't, but to my shock, she does as she's told and sits.

"You two seem to be at the center of every storm that's come through here over the last six months." Captain Warner pulls out several files and lays them on the desk in front of her. "Care to explain that?"

"We're special like that." Mattie smiles, but it's not a nice smile. It's one full of teeth. I want to kick her.

"Special?" Captain Warner cocks her head to the side. "Special wouldn't be the term I'd use to describe it."

"What she means to say is that we just were really lucky in putting two and two together."

"Yes, Richards, that I will agree with,

but my issue is how you managed to get anywhere near any of these cases. The first one, I'll give you." She glances down at the files and then back to us. "Your foster sister went missing, Miss Hathaway, and your foster mother turned out to be the perp behind several disappearances. That I'll accept as the right place, right time. But this one, I can't overlook." She holds up a file, her expression severe. "The mayor's daughter is dead. And here you two are, yet again, right in the eye of the storm."

This I hadn't expected.

"The two of them were targeting Mattie and Meg…"

She holds up a hand, stopping me. "I know that. I read the reports. I still want to know why you had whiteboards in your apartment with photocopied files of cases from several other counties. You should have brought this to my attention the moment you made the connection you did. Perhaps, had you done that, people wouldn't be dead right now."

"Perhaps he didn't tell you because he was in the hospital, suffering from a traumatic head injury that almost killed him." Mattie's eyes are narrowed, her smile almost lethal. She reminds me of her father in this moment.

"Before that…"

"And when did he have time?" Mattie leans forward, her eyes sparkling with the same arrogance I've seen mirrored in her father's. "When his mother got arrested? When he had to play referee between his parents? When you questioned him for hours about what he'd discovered about his birth mother? Let's not even talk about him having to deal with an entire family he didn't know, a family who was out for blood when it came to Ann Richards. Or perhaps when he went back to his apartment to collect his notes and all the evidence he'd compiled to bring here to you, only to be attacked and almost killed before he could? So tell me, *Captain Warner*, when did he have time to bring you up to speed?"

Captain Warner leans back and regards her with a blank expression. The cop face, I call it. I'm betting she's cursing Squirt out six ways to Sunday behind all that calm. I've never heard anyone speak to the captain like that. She terrifies most of us.

"The fact is, Dan is a great cop. He sees things where others don't. Take Sally, for instance. Officer Donut-Hole wrote her off as a runaway, when she was, in fact, a murder victim. He made connections that no one even saw. He did his research and handed you the evidence to guarantee the DA would get a conviction. Instead of sitting here blaming him for things out of his control, you should be thanking him for everything he's done to do his job despite all that's going on in his personal life."

Remind me to never piss Mattie Hathaway off.

"And how do you fit into all of this, Miss Hathaway?" Captain Warner folds her arms across her chest. "Dan, I can understand. He's a police officer. How do you fit in the puzzle?"

"I already told you. I'm just special like that."

She and Captain Warner stare each other down. The room is dead quiet until the captain opens the top file and pulls out all the sketches Mattie did for me. Those were in a folder at my apartment. Dread seeps into every pore I have. No way can either of us explain how her drawings mimic the state of the bodies as they were found, before we even had crime scene photos.

"Care to explain these?" She starts to lay them out one by one on the desk facing us.

"They're drawings."

"I can see that. Care to explain what these were doing at Richards' apartment? Some of these victims we hadn't discovered yet. We had their most recent photos, but these drawings depict their deaths. Exactly."

For once she keeps her mouth shut and just glares, defiant in the face of something that is going to bite us in the butt.

"Richards?" Captain Warner turns her attention to me. "Anything to say?"

"She's special?" I have no idea how to get out of this one.

The look the captain gives me is

enough to make me shrink back and want to hide under the proverbial rock. It's not like I can come out and say she sees ghosts and drew them the way they appeared to her. She'd arrest us on the spot.

"I can't tell you why she drew those." I look her in the eye so she knows I'm not being shady. "Isn't it enough that those drawings helped us identify victims and bring their murderers to justice?"

"I'm going to be asked to explain these, Officer Richards. If you can't give me a sufficient explanation, you'll be explaining it to people you don't want to talk to."

"I see dead people."

I groan at Mattie's flippant statement. She looks so serenely innocent, like the kid in the movie did when he said that line. Captain Warner, on the other hand, does not look impressed.

"Look, you wanted an explanation. That's the explanation I have for you. Believe it or not."

"You really want me to go to my superiors and say 'Oh, she's a ghost whisperer.' That's utterly ridiculous, young lady."

"Your grandmother died when she was seventy-two of a massive heart attack. She died at home, in her favorite dress. Purple with white flowers around the collar. Her name is Hattie and she loves streusel, but only if it's homemade. She taught you how to do a running stitch when you were nine, gave you your first diamond necklace when you were thirteen, and let you cry over Bobby when you were sixteen."

Shock, disbelief, anger…I can see her go through each different emotion as what Mattie says sinks in.

"And before you ask how I know all that, Hattie is standing right behind you. She told me. She says to tell you not to worry, Muffin, it's all going to be all right."

Muffin? The captain's grandmother called her Muffin?

"Look, lady, you don't have to believe me. I frankly don't care if you believe me or not, but you will not sit here and make accusations about Dan. He doesn't deserve it. Not after everything he went through to uncover the truth. The truth everyone else was willing to ignore."

Oh, wow. She actually told her she can see ghosts? Mattie *never* tells anyone that. Why would she say that?

Captain Warner stares mutely at her, and I can see the first faint signs of fear forming in her eyes. Not a good thing. She can make Mattie's life very unpleasant if she wants to. Although I think Mr. Crane would have something to say about that, and I don't want the captain fired.

"Captain, ma'am." I lean forward, my face as earnest as I can make it. "We came to try to help Kayla. I know this all sounds unreal, and you're probably trying to decide if we're pulling your leg or not, but we still need to find that little girl. You're a good cop. You know I wouldn't be here if I didn't think we could help."

It's several long minutes before she answers, and I'm surprised again today. I thought she'd throw us out or possibly even arrest us for interfering with a police investigation, but she doesn't do any of that.

"Tell me what you need."

***

CSU has already gone over the bear, taken samples of the bloodstains, and dusted the plastic dress the doll wore for fingerprints. They were quicker than I'd thought they'd be. Missing kid, though. It's every police officer's worst nightmare. Kelly Roberts is the crime lab tech working on the bear and all the other victims of this particular perp. She's on the phone when we come in, so Mattie and I walk over to her station to wait.

Captain Warner didn't even quibble over letting Mattie come. Today is full of surprises.

"Dan." Kelly's smile is always at one hundred percent, even in the face of all the tragedy she investigates. Like blood-soaked teddy bears. "Can I do something for you?"

"The captain has me working on the Rawlins case. I just came to see if you guys found anything, and then I thought I'd take the bear down to evidence lockup for you."

"I thought you took a leave of absence?" Kelly starts typing on her computer.

"All hands on deck with this one."

Kelly's eyes flicker to Mattie who speaks up before I can.

"I'm observing for a school project. Summer school. I'm taking a few extra classes so I can graduate early. The captain cleared it as long as I don't release any details of the case."

"That's pretty awesome." Kelly's blonde hair bounces in its ponytail when she turns to face us. "Not this case, of course, but it's great to observe police work."

Mattie puts on her most innocent smile. The girl can lie like nobody's business. She's quite scary sometimes.

"So what do we know?" I pull out my phone and bring up my notes app. It's a lot easier than trying to carry around a notebook and pen all the time.

"We type matched the blood on the

bear with the child's blood. That much is a match. I've got DNA results pending, but I think we're all confident it's her blood. The fabric makes finding any kind of useable print impossible."

"So we don't know anything new?" Not that I was expecting anything grand, but I'd hoped for at least some kind of clue.

"Well, I wouldn't say that." She looks up from the computer screen, a frown on her face. "We found traces of sulphur on the bear and some type of goo embedded in the material. I'm still running that through a chemical analysis, but so far I've gotten no hits on known substances."

"Goo?" Mattie tilts her head. "Was it black?"

"Yes. Have you seen it before?"

"No, but Kayla went missing from my neighborhood. We were there when they found the bear. I thought I saw something black on it, that's all."

Black goo. I've seen it before. While we were in New Orleans, a lower level demon attacked Mattie. It oozed that black slimy stuff. Black goo. A small shudder goes through me at the memory of that thing. It's not something I ever want to experience again. Zeke's probably right in assuming a demon is involved in all the disappearances and murders. If it holds with the same pattern, Kayla has a week to be found before she's killed.

"Did anyone check for the same substance at any of the other crime scenes?" I blink when I hear Mattie's question and refocus on the conversation. She's going to make an excellent police officer if I can just convince her to give the force a try. I know she and cops don't see eye to eye and have some bad history, but she has the instincts of a cop. I'd hate to see her waste all that potential.

Kelly frowns and goes back to her computer. After a few minutes, she shakes her head. "No mention of it in any of the other files."

"But did they know to look for it?" Mattie presses. "Maybe Kayla got in a lucky shot and some of the stuff rubbed off on the bear. Maybe there wasn't anything to find at the other locations.

But what if they overlooked it because they didn't *know* to look for it?"

"That's a very good point." Kelly squinted at her screen. "Maybe I'll send a team back to each site to look for this stuff. It can't hurt to cover all our bases."

"No, it can't." I shift, my attention on the bear sitting inconspicuously on the table in the plastic evidence bag. "If that's all, I'll go ahead and run the bear down to evidence lockup."

"We normally do that." Kelly frowns at me, clearly wondering at the break in protocol.

I shrug. "I told Captain Warner I'd do it, but if you'd rather and have the extra time, that's fine."

She purses her lips, but after a minute, she hands me the bag. The sealed bag. Now how am I going to touch the thing if it's in a sealed bag? There'll be too many questions if I open it.

"Can I see it?" Mattie leans forward, her hands outstretched and tries to take the bag from Kelly the same time I do. She pulls and the flimsy plastic tears. "Oh my gosh! I am so sorry. I didn't mean to do that. Did I ruin it?"

Kelly clucks at her like a mother hen. "No, no, sweetie. It's fine. I'll make a new one and we'll transfer it. No harm done. I need to go grab one out of the office. I used the last one I had out here earlier. Give me just a second."

She's beyond scary sometimes.

As soon as Kelly disappears, Mattie shoves the bear at me. I'm not sure how she managed to hold onto it, honestly. Kelly should have taken it with her. Chain of custody can't be broken, but I'm not going to tell on her, and there's no one else in here.

The tear is long, and half the bear is sticking out of the bag. I only have to touch it, but I don't know if I can. I know I don't want to, but Mattie's right. If I can see anything to help that little girl, then I have to at least try.

Tentatively, I brush my thumb over the soft fur and then curl my fingers around it. I'm prepared for the onslaught of images, but nothing comes. Frowning, I clutch it tighter. It's just an ordinary bear.

"I got nothing."

"Really?" Mattie pushes in closer. "Let's try something. Close your eyes and think about earlier. Think about when we pulled up to the driveway. Think about Kayla standing there, playing. Concentrate on that image, on what she was wearing, on her face, her expressions. Think about nothing but Kayla and the last time you saw her."

Sensory memories. The eye sees more than it can process all at once. It's a technique used in a lot of law enforcement branches to help a witness recover memories they didn't even realize they had. It almost always works.

I close my eyes and allow my mind to wander back to this morning. I can see her there in her yard, her blonde hair and blue eyes watching the car. She probably didn't recognize the car and was curious. Kayla is cute. I remember thinking I wanted to check to see how many registered sex offenders lived in the area. Kids that cute tend to attract unwanted attention. Always good to have an idea about those kinds of things.

I got out of the car and she grinned at

Mattie, then went back to playing with her bear when Mary flew out of the house. I could just see her out of the corner of my eye as we talked to Mary. Playing by the fence. The street only had a couple of cars, but none of them set off alarm bells. We followed Mary up the porch steps, and I glanced back one more time. Still in her yard. I turned my head back toward the door and…there. Across the street. I see him. Jeans and a sweatshirt hoodie. He's not supposed to be there. Out of place.

A flickering starts behind my eyes, just blurry bits and pieces at first. Kayla talking to the bear, making plans for a tea party. She hears a noise and looks up. She sees the man standing outside the gate right in front of her. Fear. The stench of sulphur. I see him. Only it's like I'm seeing two people. Like I got hit with a baseball right in the face and I'm seeing double. That can't be right, can it?

She's afraid and tries to run, only he's ready. I see him grab a fistful of her hair with one hand and yank her up very fast, his other hand covering her mouth. Pain.

Stinging, searing pain.

I can see the long cuts on her arms. The fence. She cut her arm on the fence. The blood ran down and onto the bear. She tried to hold onto it as he dragged her over the fence and hustled her down the street, but her arm hurt too much, and she dropped it. That's how it got blood on it.

More images flood my field of vision. So fast I can't make sense of them, so fast I get dizzy. I reach out and grasp the edge of the counter I'm standing beside to keep from falling.

"Let go of it, Dan."

Mattie's voice is faint, but it's enough to cut through the cacophony of images, and I let the bear drop to the floor, and they stop. Gone. Like they weren't even there. Three deep, shuddering breaths later, I bend down and pick up the bear, only this time, I keep hold of the plastic bag. Not touching that thing again.

Kelly breezes back in, evidence bag in hand. She takes one look at my face, and concern wipes the smile off hers. "Dan, are you all right? You look like you're about to pass out."

"I told him to take it easy." Mattie wrings her hands, and only some of it is for show. She's worried about me. I see it in her eyes. "The hospital wanted to keep him for observation this morning, but he insisted he was fine. He's not. He gets dizzy spells and can barely stand up."

"I think I'd better take this down to evidence." Kelly takes the bear from me, and I don't protest. "You need to go sit down and rest for a while."

"Thanks." I attempt a smile, but my lips won't quite curl up. Flashes of what I'd seen keep interrupting. I do need to sit and work through everything.

Mattie hovers as we walk to the elevators. It's hard for her to not demand to know everything, but she's getting better at restraint. This is not the place to talk about it. It's not until we're in the car that she turns and gives me an expectant look tinged with worry.

"I don't think we're dealing with a demon." I roll the window up and turn the air on. It's over a hundred degrees outside. I know she'll cut the AC off in a few minutes, but I'll bask while I can.

"Well, maybe we are."

"Which is it?" She starts the car and backs out of the parking spot. "Either it's a demon or it's not."

"Well, I think it's a man who's being influenced by a demon." I tell her about everything I'd seen while she pulls out into traffic and shifts lanes so we can get back on I-77. "What do you think?"

"I think we need to talk to Doc." The grouchy ire in each word is enough to tell me she'd rather eat juicy worms than call Dr. Olivet. I'm not the only one making concessions.

Chapter Fifteen

Mattie

We didn't make it to Doc's. Eli called and said his mom wanted us to come over. Dan was not happy about letting Eli anywhere near me, but like I told him, tough. He was going to have to deal with it. I do understand his hesitation. He saw the same deaths I did, or at least that last one. His first instinct is to protect me, so is Eli's. He's my freaking Guardian Angel, for crying out loud. I don't think he can hurt me.

Dan's not betting on that being the case, though.

We've been sitting in the Malones' driveway for at least two minutes. Dan's staring up at the house like it's a wild, rabid dog. His trepidation isn't all about me, and he knows it. This is his family's home. The family he'd been robbed of.

His past is just as screwed up as mine. Ann Richards and my mother, Claire Hathaway, had been sisters. Claire's real name is Amanda Sterling, but to me, she's always going to be Claire. Ann and Claire discovered that the Malones were special, that they could see ghosts and went about dealing with the bad ones. Ann thought of them as evil and "rescued" Dan from them. The way she did it is why she ended up in jail. She kidnapped Dan's birth mother, held her hostage until she gave birth, and then killed her.

Dan discovered all this while helping me try to find my father. He also found his own birth father in the process, John Malone. With him came a ready-made family in the form of three new brothers and a sister. Dan still isn't quite prepared to deal with them. Not that I blame him. It'd be a shock to anyone. I only have a father and grandparents to deal with, and a possible brother somewhere, but if I was faced with an entire family of strangers? Not sure I wouldn't just pick up and run again.

"You sure about this, Squirt?" He squints up at the front door when it opens. His baby brother, Benny, darts out and runs out to the car.

"I don't think Benny cares if I am or not." I don't wait for Dan to change his mind. I get out of the car and walk around to greet the little boy. He's adorable with Eli's aqua eyes, but otherwise, he looks just like Dan and Caleb.

Dan is much slower in getting out, but when he does, Benny lunges at him, wrapping him in a bear hug, and Dan ruffles his hair. "Hey there, little guy."

"You lived!" The little boy looks up, tears in his eyes. "I thought you might die."

"Nah." Dan hugs the kid back. "I think Mattie would beat me if I died on her."

Benny nods, his expression grave. "She's got a mean right hook. Gotta be careful around that one."

I can't help but laugh at how serious he is. Such a cute kid. "Don't worry, kid. You're safe around me. I only hit people at least as big as me."

He eyeballs me with cynicism, but latches onto Dan's hand and starts pulling him up the drive toward the porch. I follow along behind them, doing my best not to laugh at Dan's expression. It's part mirth, part panic. The boy needs to buck up.

The house is what I call cookie cutter. They've moved into one of the nicer neighborhoods in the university area, but there are only so many designs. All the houses are basically the same. No uniqueness at all. And with the homeowner's association, you can only do so much when it comes to colors. Blah, I say.

It is nice, though. Well, it will be once it's all unpacked. Boxes are everywhere. They only recently moved here, and I guess with everything going on, finding time to unpack hasn't been easy.

The more I look, the more I realize a lot of the boxes are new. Even furniture boxes. I remember Eli telling me when they moved, they literally moved with no furniture. No wonder it's taking them a while. I'm betting they bought all new furniture and are now trying to put it together. Not a fun thing.

"Hilda."

I turn to see Eli standing by the kitchen island. He looks worried. Those gorgeous eyes of his are shining with something akin to fear, and it sets my hackles rising.

"Eli Malone, if those dishes aren't loaded, I swear you are going to be on kitchen duty for a month!"

We all turn to see a woman descending the stairs, a clothes basket overflowing with dirty laundry in front of her. She's very petite, her brown hair brushed back over her shoulder. Dan moves back so she doesn't run him over. When she finally looks up at the bottom of the stairs, she stops, nonplussed.

"Dan's here, Mama." Benny beams up at her, his hand still wrapped around Dan's. "And the ghost girl who punched out Eli."

He had to go there, didn't he? He had

to remind their mother I decked her son?

Heather Malone turns to look at me, but instead of hostility, I'm met with laughter. "He probably deserved it."

"Hey!" Eli stalks over. "I did not deserve it. I was only trying to help her."

"You grabbed me in a dark room without so much as a hello." I give him my best grin. "You deserved it."

He winks and pulls me away from Dan, his arm sliding around me. "Mom, this Hilda and Dan."

"And that's why you get hit. How many times do I have to tell you not to call me Hilda?" The ire in my voice belies the warm fuzzy feeling being in his arms gives me. I wish I could trust this was something more than the bond we share.

"Mattie, Dan, I am so happy to finally get to meet you both." She looks torn about if she should attempt to hug us or shake hands or simply go about her business. "I just wish it were under better circumstances." Her eyes flicker to Eli who ignores her completely and pulls me closer.

Dan's entire body tenses up like he's gearing up to tackle Eli, and before I can say a word, Heather stares her son down. "Eli, I don't think that's a good idea."

"Mom, this is stupid," he grumbles, but lets me go. "I'm not going to hurt her."

His mother knows something, and it's frightened her enough to warn Eli away from me. This can't be good at all.

"Probably not, but until we can figure out how to break the curse, the safest thing to do is stay away from her."

"Curse?" Dan slides closer to me. I can feel his stress level go up another notch. He so does not need this right now. We have enough to worry about with all the murdered kids.

Heather shakes her head. "Let me put this down, and then we all need to sit down and talk. Benny, go to your room and play for a little while."

"Grown up stuff?" He wrinkles his nose in disgust.

"Yes, grown up stuff." She moves around us and goes toward the kitchen.

Eli glares after her retreating back. "I'm not going to hurt you."

"I know." I try to sound reassuring, but I don't think I manage it, because he only glares at me and then stalks off after his mom.

"You won't leave without saying goodbye?" Benny tugs on Dan's hand to get his attention.

"I promise." Dan ruffles his hair and the kid dashes up the stairs like he's got fire under his feet. Where do they get all that energy?

We shuffle into the kitchen where Eli's mom is waiting. She waves us to sit then pulls out three very old looking books, one of which is massive. "Since Eli told us about your vision of Harper and my ancestor, I've been poring over family tomes looking for anything about it. What I've discovered is very unsettling. When Eli told me the men in your visions have his color eyes, it set off an alarm bell. I remember my grandmother telling me a very old story about a man in our family who became cursed. I've been searching all morning, and I finally found the story."

She flips the largest of the books open

and thumbs through the pages until she finds what she's looking for. "Here. It directly relates to Harper and Captain Hiller."

The Civil War couple. I remember them vividly.

"As you know, my family has been recordkeepers for centuries, but some of my family actually dealt with the supernatural themselves. Captain Hiller was one of them. He got involved in hunting down a witch. It was why he was at that ball. The witch was a woman named Tara Bensworth. She was the daughter of one of the Sterlings' closest friends. He was there for an introduction."

"And Harper threw a wrench in the mix?" Sounds about like her. She was a feisty girl, and her mother had been intent on making sure she and Captain Hiller spent some time together.

"Yes." Heather smiled, still reading what was in front of her. "He definitely got thrown for a loop when he met Harper. It also derailed his plans. His mission was to get close to the witch, close enough that he could stop her."

"Close enough to make her fall for him?" I am beginning to see where this is going and how it could end very, very badly. Girl meets boy, girl falls in love with boy, only to discover boy loves someone else. Add in the fact he wanted to kill her? She probably wanted him to suffer something awful.

Heather nods. "And he did exactly that. He kept the relationships secret from them both, but eventually Harper discovered what was going on. She refused to see him again, thinking he'd betrayed her. The good captain, according the story, climbed up the trellis and through her window where he confessed the truth of his mission to her."

"A grand gesture." Dan nods approvingly.

"Yes," Heather agrees. "Captain Hiller decided that enough was enough and went to carry out his plan to kill the witch, only she'd found out about Harper. She'd come to the Sterling home that day with her mother and had seen the captain climb into Harper's room. She'd snuck upstairs and heard the entire conversation."

"So of course, she made her own plans." I shift, leaning forward, fascinated by the story even if it was a little predictable. Love and revenge are the two things in this world that will never change.

Heather nods, her attention solely on the story she's reading from. "Hurt and inconsolable, she crafted a curse. A curse that cannot be broken."

"Can't?" I squeak, looking to Eli. I am beginning to understand his frustration.

"She poured her soul into it, made it with pieces of her own flesh and blood to bind the dark magic. She made sure that he and his descendants would suffer the same pain he'd caused her. She felt like he'd murdered her heart, and the curse twisted that. Every single man or woman born with those eyes would murder the person they loved the most in this world, just as Tara herself was."

"Did the captain kill Tara?" Dan leans back, listening with the same curiosity I am.

"Yes, he did, but not before she cursed him." Her gaze lands on Eli who returns it with one of his own, one full of defiance. "Two years later, after their son had his first birthday, Captain Hiller stabbed Harper to death. Something came over him, the story tells. All he'd say at first when asked why he'd done it was because he loved her. A few hours later, his reality crashed and he felt the same pain he'd caused Tara."

"They all say that in my dreams, because he loves her."

"That's why I think you and Eli shouldn't be around each other." Heather looks me directly in the eyes. "It's too dangerous. He'd never forgive himself if he hurt you."

"But the curse makes them kill the people they love." I tilt my head, thinking. "Eli and I barely know each other."

"Hilda's right. I mean, I like her, but I don't think it's love. At least not yet."

"Your bond *mimics* love," Heather clarifies. "You will do anything to protect her as you are meant to do, Eli. The curse sees this as an act of love, and it's confused. Whether you love her or not is irrelevant. The curse thinks you do."

I knew this freaking bond was messing things up. The attraction was too fast, too all consuming. I mean, I do like Eli. A lot. Enough that I'm willing to see if there's something real there or not.

"So how does this curse decide when to activate?" Dan moves so he's standing between me and Eli. I roll my eyes at his back. Eli isn't about to attack me now. So overprotective. Sweet, though.

"That is part of our problem. No one can agree upon the when." Heather sighs heavily, her frustration evident.

"What do you think, Mom?" Eli sits at the table, giving up on trying to get near me. "You're good at the research stuff. You have to have a theory by now."

"Of course I do, but it's just a theory." She shuffles through a few more pages.

Dan shrugs. "That's all police work is, really. Taking what you know and making good guesses. A theory is as good as anything right now."

"From everything I've read, I think it's

the moment when he realizes how much he truly loves her."

"They were married with a son." Why hadn't I remembered that sooner?

"That makes sense." Heather nods, thinking. "In order to keep the curse alive, they'd need an heir. It was how Tara ensured its sustainability."

"But wouldn't they just stop getting married?" Eli rests his forearms on the table. "I mean, if this is what happens, why would he do that?"

Heather stares down at the book she has open like she wants to commit literary homicide. "Maybe they thought they could find a way to beat it or that it wasn't true to begin with? I just don't know, honey."

Eli shoots a hooded glance my way. "Well, how do we fix it?"

"We don't. It's powerful magic and would require powerful magic to break it. Magic that requires a blood sacrifice."

"What, like voodoo or something?" Zeke is fond of voodoo priests. He told me he wanted to consult one about how to fix my ghost energy problem. Usually you salt the doors and windows to keep the ghosts out, but it now keeps me out as well. I have too much ghost energy…but, maybe not anymore since I'm not carrying around Eric's soul. We're so going to test that theory!

"Or something." Heather's expression darkens. "It's the most ancient form of blood magic that's ever been referenced. To break this spell, you'd need a human sacrifice, and none of us are willing to do that."

"There's always a work around, Mom. We'll figure it out."

The look on his mother's face is enough to convince me that's not about to happen any time soon. There isn't a work around for this, no matter how much Eli wants there to be.

"We can be Skype buddies." I try to keep my voice upbeat because he looks so depressed. "Virtual dating is the new thing, don't you know?"

Before he can respond, the front door opens and Ava comes in, throwing her purse down while kicking off her shoes. "Who's here? I don't know the car in the driveway."

"Hey, Ava."

Her head snaps around at the sound of Dan's voice. She blinks rapidly several times. "Dan? What are you doing here? Shouldn't you be at home resting or something?"

"I'm all good." He waves off her concerns. "Your mom asked us to come over and talk about this curse business."

"No, you're not all good." I smack him in the arm when he rolls his eyes at me. A bad habit of mine he's picked up. "You just went back to the hospital and left again against doctor's wishes. You are most definitely not okay."

"*You did what*?" Ava shouts, her expression morphing from concern to outright anger faster than I can blink.

"It's not that big a deal." Dan's tone is so casual it sounds flippant, which only makes Ava's anger ratchet up another notch.

"You don't think it's a big deal?" She stalks closer, her finger wagging. "You almost died, Dan. Do you understand that? You get a second chance. Why would you throw that away by ignoring the doctors?"

"My CT was clear." He runs his fingers through his hair. "Really, I'm fine, Ava."

Instead of yelling at him again, she turns her flashing brown eyes on me, and I take a step back at the hostility in them. "He's an idiot, but you're not. Why would you let him do something like this?"

"He is an idiot," I agree, "but I can't force him to stay in the hospital. The best I can do is watch him and make sure I'm there if he needs me."

I'm actually quite proud of myself because I didn't blow up at her for shouting at me. Small steps to adulthood, I guess.

"Where's Caleb and Mr. Malone?" I steer the conversation away from Dan. Idiot he might be, but he doesn't need the stress of dealing with Ava's misplaced anger. She's scared and letting her anger control her emotions. "We need to talk to them about the murdered children."

"They're at the last abduction site." Eli

gets up and pours himself a glass of water. "Dad wanted to visit each abduction and body recovery site to look for clues the crime scene unit might have missed. He dragged Caleb with him."

"He's not gonna be home for a while, then?"

"No." Heather straightens, closing the monster book. "They should be home in a few hours, though. Why don't you two stay for dinner and…"

Dan's shaking his head before she can finish the sentence. "We have to get going. Mattie's grandparents are flying up from New Orleans, and I promised I'd get her back before too long."

He made no such promise. The whole family situation must freak him out more than I'd thought.

"But you just got here," Ava complains.

"No, they've been here for a while, Ava. Had you been home early like I'd asked you to, you could have spent some time with your brother."

I know that tone of voice. Mrs. Cross has used it on Mary and me several times. Ava's in for it.

"We really do need to go. Can someone find Ben? I promised not to leave without saying goodbye."

"Are you always so proper?" Ava avoids eye contact with her mother and turns her attention to Dan.

He smiles. "My mom pretty much drilled proper manners into me and Cam before we could talk, I think. She's a stickler for that."

The room goes deathly quiet at the mention of Ann Richards, and Dan realizes what he'd said in the next second. "I'm sorry, I…"

"No." Heather puts her hand on his arm. "She's your mother, Dan. Don't apologize for that. It may be uncomfortable for us to talk about, but don't feel like you need to walk on eggshells over that fact."

"Thank you."

I wasn't expecting that from her. She seems really nice, a good mom, but even nice people have their breaking points. I wasn't sure how she'd handle Dan's mom. Everyone else seems to ignore the elephant in the room, but not Heather. She seems to understand he loves his mother. My respect for her just went up five notches.

Ava goes to collect Benny, and I wander outside to wait on Dan. Our next stop is Zeke's. Grandparents.

"Finally."

Eli slides in next to me, his arms pulling me into him. I figured he'd sneak out here. My belly does that crazy flip-flop thing and I snuggle into him. This feels so good, to be in his arms, so perfect. That's why I'm so suspicious of it. Nothing should feel this perfect. For the minute, I ignore my doubts and bask in the warmth of Eli.

"I missed you." I lay my head on his chest and listen to the sound of his heart.

"I missed you too, Hilda." His chin nestles in my hair and he pulls me closer. "You know I won't hurt you, don't you?"

How to answer that? After everything I've seen, I know there is a good possibility he might. "Eli, I know you wouldn't want to, but if that curse activates, you won't have a choice. I've seen what it does to the men in your family."

"I'm your Guardian Angel, Mattie. My job is to protect you. I couldn't hurt you if I wanted to." He sounds so desperate to believe that. "I swear I won't hurt you."

I know he'd try his best not to hurt me, but that curse is some nasty business. I'm betting none of the others thought they'd hurt their loved ones either.

"I knew it!"

The sound of his mother's voice makes us jump apart. We turn to see her coming down the porch steps, disapproval stamped all over her face. She's carrying two books with her.

"Mom…"

"Don't 'Mom' me, young man! You promised to stay away from her…"

"I did no such thing!" He stands straight and faces his mother. "You just demanded I stay away from her. I never promised to."

"Then I want you to promise me that right here and now." Her aqua eyes flash with a deep and unbridled fear under the mask of anger. I can see how terrified she is, even if Eli can't.

"I'm her Guardian Angel. How am I supposed to protect her if I can't get near her?"

"Your mom's right, Eli."

He turns to look at me, angry and confused. "Hilda…"

"No." I shake my head. "This curse? It's too dangerous. If she's right about this bond mimicking love, then what happens when I'm in serious danger and it kicks in? I've been that girl who died at her husband's hands in my dreams. I've felt myself get stabbed and shot. Felt her confusion, her betrayal. Her pain. If you hurt me like that, you'd never forgive yourself. Dan would never forgive you either. The two of you get a second chance. I won't let you risk everything just to be near me. I do care about you, Eli. It's why I'm saying your mom's right. You have to stay away from me until we can figure this out."

He looks like I just sucker punched him in the gut. "I'm sorry, Eli, but you know I'm right."

I expect him to get mad and storm off,

but instead, he pulls me against him and kisses me. Desperation. I can feel all the desperate longing in his kiss, feel it in the way I cling to him.

When he lets me go, I take a shaky breath and try to steady myself. Eli's kisses always have that effect on me. Without a word, he stomps up the steps and inside, leaving both his mother and me staring after him.

"Thank you for that." Heather sighs deeply. "I know he hates this, but I'm only trying to protect him. It has nothing to do with you. From everything I've been told, you're a great person, Mattie. I don't want to hurt either of you."

"I know." And I do know. She's just being a mom.

"I wanted to show you these." She hands me the two books she's holding. "They are part of my family's journals and talk about living reapers. I thought it might help you understand who you are and what it all means. I'd planned on letting you read through them while here, but it doesn't look like that's going to be a possibility in the near future. You need to know this, so I'm willing to let you borrow them."

"Really?" Wow. She's willing to let me borrow something so valuable?

"Of course." She smiles, and for the first time, the fear and worry are erased from her face. "John's family has been tasked with protecting living reapers from the beginning. My family didn't come across that little fact until about a hundred years ago, but once we did, we researched it heavily. I hope these books can help you understand who you are a little better."

I take the books from her. The leather is old and soft. "These books feel so old. I won't hurt them by reading them, will I?"

"No, they're protected from aging with a simple spell."

Magic. Of course. I keep forgetting magic is real. I have enough runes tattooed into my flesh to be a constant reminder, but they're in places I can't see, so I don't remember them.

"Like the runes they tattooed on me?"

Heather laughs. "They called them

runes, did they? They're not true runes. The designs are ancient, derived from some of the runes history teaches us about, but the symbols are mostly for show. The magic is in the ink, the spell worked in as they ink you."

That makes more sense than some kind of supernatural hoodoo symbols. I can buy that the ink is spelled and the magic transferred over into the tattoo more than I can it being just the symbols working without any help.

"Get these back to me when you're done with them, please. I'll go inside and send Dan out. I know you need to get going. And, Mattie, thank you for putting your foot down with Eli. You didn't have to."

"Yeah, I did. I meant it when I said I care about him. I don't want him to get hurt either."

"I think you might hurt him anyway." She bites her lip, a debate in her eyes.

"What do you mean?"

"Dan." She gives me a sad, knowing smile. "I've seen the way you look at him and the way he looks at you. I don't think my son would stand a chance if it wasn't for this bond. He's going to get his heart broken. So, please, before you go any further with him, think about what you really want. If it's Dan, then let Eli know that."

"I…"

She shakes her head. "You don't know it yourself, Mattie, but you're in love with Dan. You could very easily fall in love with my son because of this bond. If that happens, you're going to hurt one of them very badly. None of you deserve that kind of pain. So think about how you really feel and make up your mind before this gets out of control."

She gives me this sad little smile and walks away, leaving me reeling.

She thinks I'm in love with Dan?

No, she can't be right. Dan and I already had this discussion. We decided that we got confused about our feelings. He loved Meg. I accepted that. I didn't like it, but I accepted it.

But did I? The idea of him with Meg still sets my teeth to gnashing. It's more than her being my best friend and promising not to make a move on him until I figured out my feelings. Sure, I was pissed she'd broken her word, but it was more than that. It hurt me to the point I could barely breathe. I mean, I ran all the way to New Orleans and right smack dab into a haunted house to get away from the pain of them being together.

And then I met Eli. We had this crazy insane attraction that buried the pain of Meg and Dan being together. Eli is hard to explain. I like him. So much. He makes me burn with this intense desire, and he gives me butterflies in my stomach. Dan never did that. With Eli, it's easy as breathing. Dan is complicated, hard, but the thought of losing him sends me into a panic so severe, it's like I'm trapped under something, crushing my chest, and I can't breathe. The thought of losing Eli doesn't do that to me.

The more I think about it, the more confused I become. Maybe I need to stay away from them both until I figure this out. Time and distance. Dan has a lot on his plate right now, anyway, with his mom and getting to know the Malones. That's not going to work, though. I know Dan. If I try to push him away, he'll dig in deeper. I tried that once already, and I got my butt chewed out. Like he says, he's in it for the long haul. He won't leave me, and he won't let me leave him.

We're stuck with each other for better or for worse.

Chapter Sixteen

Thirty minutes later we are pulling into the parking garage of Zeke's apartment complex. We've both been quiet on the ride over. Dan looks lost and a little pissed off. The last twenty-four hours have been excessively hard on him. Losing Meg, discovering he came back from the ghost plane with psychic ability...it's all a bit much for a guy who never used to believe in something unless he could physically see and touch it. Science. That was his religion. Now he has to deal with ghosts, angels, demons, and who knows what else.

I switch the ignition off and turn to him. "You okay?"

"Peachy."

That's one of my lines. "Seriously, Dan, are you okay? You scared me earlier when your nose started to bleed, and you're recovering from shock, and..."

He puts a finger to my lips. "Shush. I'm fine."

"You're not fine, Dan."

He leans his head against the headrest. "No, I'm not fine, but I will be. I have to be."

"No, you don't have to be. After everything you've gone through, no one expects you to be fine. You need to take a minute and let yourself not be fine."

He doesn't say anything to me as he gets out of the car. Conversation over, I guess. Frustrated, I get out of the car, lock it, and follow Dan to the elevator. While we wait for the doors to open, I study him. He's tired, worn, and a little pale. Rest. That's what he needs.

"Stop staring at me like I'm going to flip out."

"I'm not."

He rounds on me. "Yeah, you are, Mattie. Just stop, okay?"

"You need a nap."

"What?"

"A nap." I nod. Yup, that's the best for Mr. Grouchy. "Maybe then you'll get over this burr in your bonnet and stop snapping at me for worrying about you."

"Bee in your bonnet," he mutters.

"What?" What's he going on about now?

"It's not a burr in your bonnet. It's a bee in your bonnet."

"Whatever. Means the same thing."

He shakes his head and jabs the elevator button again, like he's eager to get away from me, which hurts.

"Why are you so pissed at me?"

"I'm not."

"You are, Officer Dan, and I don't know why."

"Mattie…"

"Don't lie to me because you're mad. What did I do?"

He closes his eyes, every tense muscle screaming frustration. "Leave it alone, Mattie."

Leave it alone? When has he ever left it alone when I asked him to? Never.

"Nope, you are going to tell me what's going on so we can fix it."

When he opens those brown eyes of his, they aren't full of anger like I'd expected. Instead they burn with an intent, and I'm not prepared when I find myself pinned against the wall and his lips crashing down onto mine.

It's not like with Eli; there isn't this explosive fire. It's a slow burn that starts where his lips are on mine and then travels down every nerve ending I have. Engulfed. That's what it feels like. I'm engulfed in a fire that burns hot enough to chase away the cold in my bones, hot enough to scorch away the bitter pain of every bad thing that's ever happened to me. But beneath all that heat, is this feeling of contentment, of safety and peace that fills every jagged hole in my heart. I'd thought Eli felt like home, but I didn't really understand what home was. Not until now.

I stop fighting the sensation and relax, my lips moving with his in our own little dance. Heat, desire, love. All those things wrap around me when he deepens the kiss, pushing against me until there isn't even the barest of millimeters separating our bodies. Who needs butterflies when there is this? I can't even define what it feels like, all I know is I want more and reach up, twining my fingers in his hair. This kiss is the kind of kiss I've only ever read about. This kiss is the stuff of legends.

The elevator doors open, and the couple inside gasp, tearing the two of us apart. We step aside and let them exit the elevator before boarding it ourselves.

"Why did you do that?" My fingers press lightly against my bruised lips. Maybe it was a kneejerk reaction to him losing Meg? He's not thinking straight.

"Because it's something I've wanted to do since I met you." He closes his eyes and lets out a soul wrenching sigh. "I'm not mad at you, Mattie. I'm mad at *me*."

"You're mad about kissing me?"

"No, never that." He blinks his eyes open and looks at me. "I saw Eli kiss you, and it all boiled over, and I realized something. I'm mad at myself because every time I try to think about Meg, all I can think about is you. Last night, when I heard those shots fired, my girlfriend, who I did love, was the last person on my mind. When I saw you both take a bullet, all I saw was you. I could lose Meg, but I couldn't lose you. I'm mad at myself because I should be more broken up about Meg dying, but I can't be because you're safe. And that means more to me than anything or anyone else. I'm mad at me because I convinced myself to stay away from you because of your age, because you needed a friend more than you needed another guy in your life. I'm mad at myself because I should have told you all this before Meg, before Eli…I'm just mad, Mattie."

Is he trying to tell me what I think he is? My mouth drops open, and before I can say a word, the elevator doors open and he's rushing out, leaving me staring after him. Did Dan Richards just tell me he loves me in his own weird way?

I stand there for a full minute, long enough for the elevator doors to shut on me. Memories of the morgue elevator are enough to have me smashing the open button and hightailing it out of there. Dan's already gone inside, and Zeke's poking his head out to look for me.

"Everything okay?"

"Fine," I mutter and dodge around him. "Been a long day."

"It's about to get longer." He closes the door behind me. "My parents are here."

Great, just freaking great. My head's still reeling from Dan and his earth-shattering kiss, and I have to deal with grandparents now? Fate must hate me or has a sick, twisted sense of humor.

"I need to get cleaned up. We've spent all morning looking for a missing kid, and I stink. Where's Dan?"

"He went upstairs to his room, I think. Missing child?"

"The little girl who lives next door to the Crosses disappeared out of her yard this morning. We've been walking for miles looking for her."

Zeke frowns. "I hope it's not connected to the murders."

"It's connected." I explain to him about the bear and the stench of sulphur. "There's a lot more I want to talk to you about too, but if your parents are here, I really need a shower before I meet them."

"Of course, *ma petite*. Mrs. Banks went out shopping earlier, and you'll find some clean clothes in your bathroom."

Thank you, Mrs. Banks. I don't waste any more time and rush up the stairs. I so do not want to meet his parents looking like the mess I do. I'm already terrified they'll think I'm not good enough for their fancy family. Despite Zeke's assurances, I might come up lacking because of how I grew up. Even if my father doesn't want to admit it, it's a distinct possibility.

Dan's door is firmly shut when I round the corner. I want to barge in and demand to finish our conversation, but the word *grandparents* flashes like warning lights in mind. I need to deal with them first. It takes me all of ten minutes to shower, but at least a good twenty minutes is wasted while I try to tame my hair. Curls are awful when you don't have time to make them relax.

Mrs. Banks got me jeans and a green t-shirt. She didn't go for a dress or anything fancy. Just normal clothes. I love her the tiniest bit more as I hustle myself into the soft fabric. Old Navy. I always loved their clothes, though I typically do all my shopping at Walmart. Foster care only pays for so much.

I give myself a once over and decide I look about as presentable as I can, never mind the wild look in my eyes. Nothing to be done about that. I don't run down the stairs. For once, I take my time. I'd hoped Dan would be here with me when I met these people, but I can deal on my own. Not the first time and not the last time I've been in these situations by myself.

I've gotten so dependent on Dan, sometimes I forget I can do stuff on my own. I'm a strong, independent woman. I don't need anyone to save me or be there for me when I'm in a difficult situation. Don't get me wrong, having someone there is nice, but I don't *need* them. I'm Mattie Louise Hathaway. I can do this.

I can hear the soft murmur of voices coming from Zeke's office. I stop a few feet from the closed door. What if they don't like me? What if they don't approve of me? I mean, I don't have their manners, their upbringing. I grew up poor, and they were rolling in dough. Every stereotype known to man about the rich and the poor plays out in my head. All the what-ifs are enough to drive me nuts. I don't want to embarrass Zeke. He's been so good to me, and he loves me. Really loves me. If it were just the two of us, it'd be all good, but I have to deal with everyone in his world.

And that's the problem. I don't know how to fit in that world. I'm not a part of it. I'm just me. Mattie Louise Hathaway, foster kid.

"They don't bite, you know."

I jump at the sound of Jamison's voice. Zeke's butler is sneakier than I am. No one can usually get the jump on me, but I never heard him creeping up.

"I know." I try to squash the irritation in my voice. He's only trying to help.

"They're going to love you, Miss Mattie. Stop fretting about it and go meet your family."

"Are you always this bossy?" I scuff

my tennis shoe, buying more time.

He laughs. "Only when I have to be. Come on, I'll announce you."

See, there's another difference. In Zeke's world, you're announced when you enter a room. In my world, you just go in and say hi. It's all these little differences that are going to be the death of me and my confidence.

Jamison doesn't give me time to procrastinate any more. He walks to the door, knocks, and opens it. I hear him mumble something that includes my name. Then he stands aside and looks back at me expectantly, a twinkle in his eyes. I'm so going to get even, and the dirty look I give him sings that promise in spades. His response? A wink.

When I duck into the room, the first person I see is Zeke. He's standing by his desk directly in front of me. His eyes are reassuring, but I can't stop the nerves in my stomach from making me all queasy.

A woman comes around the desk, stopping beside him, her smile plastered from ear to ear. She doesn't look much older than forty, but that can't be right, can it? I mean, his mom would need to be in her sixties or something. This woman is tall, her dark brown hair cut fashionably short and styled to perfection. She's wearing a dark blue dress and heels, pearls adorning her neck and earlobes. She looks very sophisticated. Not at all grandmotherly.

The man who's standing by the fireplace is more along the lines of what I think a grandfather should look like. He's tall, like Zeke, his salt and pepper hair only adding to his distinguished profile. Unlike his wife, he's dressed more casually in slacks and a button down shirt. More approachable. The wife looks like she'd claw your eyes out if you so much as smudged her very expensive shoes.

"Mama, Papa, this is Mattie." Zeke's voice shines with pride, and it helps bolster up my sudden plunge of self-confidence. I'm slightly terrified of the woman who's staring me down. Usually, I'd be all up in her face, but I don't want to embarrass my father who has been nothing but be accepting of me. "These are your grandparents. Lila and Josiah Crane."

Josiah approaches me first, a hesitant smile on his face. "You don't know how long we've waited to meet you. We wanted to come down last week, but Zeke refused to let us. We were ready to come anyway." Josiah winks conspiratorially at me. "We're his parents, and he can't boss us."

I have a feeling Zeke bosses pretty much who he pleases.

"Look at you, so grown up. And as beautiful as your mother." He doesn't ask me, he just hugs me. So un-Zeke-like. I go stiff in his arms, unsure what to do. Do I hug him back? I look helplessly to Zeke, whose only response is to grin.

"Stop hogging my granddaughter, Josiah Crane." Lila's voice is soft, cultured, and has a definite southern drawl. Not at all uppity, though. She sounds happy to see me.

The old man hugs me tighter for a moment and leans down. "We are so glad to have you home." When he releases me, I can see the tears in his eyes. He's doing his best to hold them at bay.

"Come here, young lady." Lila's voice is a command that's expected to be followed. I don't do so well with commands, though. Instead of rolling over to her, I turn so I can face her.

Zeke laughs. "I forgot to tell you she has my stubborn streak, Mama. She's as good at following orders as me too."

"God help us," Lila mutters. "One of you is enough to give me gray hairs." She walks over to me, her heels clicking on the hardwood floors. Her eyes are hazel, like mine. We even have the same shade of brown in our hair. At first I thought it came from my birth mother, but looking at Lila, I can see similarities between us. She still looks young enough to be my mother and not my grandmother. Good genes, maybe?

"Let me look at you." Lila walks in a circle around me, and its sets my teeth to grinding. I am not livestock waiting to be inspected by the next bidder. "Well, you look a little worse for the wear, but being shot will do that to you."

"It only nicked me."

"Nicked or not, gunshot wounds are serious. I swear, when Ezekiel told me you'd been shot last night, I didn't know if my heart would take it. Don't do that to us, child. We lost you once, we can't lose you again."

The raw emotion in her voice makes me look up. Her hazel eyes are bright with unshed tears. "Can I hug you?"

Zeke nods encouragingly.

"Sure." I try to sound upbeat, but it comes out more like a cross between dread and 'I'd rather be shot than hug you.'

"I know we're strangers to you, Mattie." It comes out Mahyatee. So odd hearing my name drawn out like that.

"Yes, you are." I nod. "I don't mean to be mean or standoffish, and I'm sure you're really nice people, but I don't know you, and…" I shrug, unable to put what I'm feeling into words. It's different than it was with Zeke. As soon as he hugged me, I felt this connection. I knew he loved me, and that was all I needed. But grandparents? A whole cat of a different color. I have trust issues. I can't help it.

"Sugar, you take all the time you need to get to know us. We're your family, and there's no getting rid of us any time soon. Just ask your father. I make him call me every Sunday, and he's a grown man with a teenager." Her smile is infectious.

Lila Crane is probably one of the kindest souls I've ever encountered, despite her outward appearance. I can see this bright blue haze surround her when she talks about her family. I know she deals in demons, but that doesn't diminish the love and affection she has for them. For me.

I understand in that second she loves me. She loves me as much as she does Zeke. I can't say I love her back, but it does give me a warm, fuzzy feeling. Enough so that I hug her unexpectedly and she never hesitates. She wraps her arms around me and hugs me until all I can smell is her fruity perfume. Oranges. She smells like oranges, like me.

She leans back and regards me with the most serious expression I've seen on anyone's face. "We wanted you when you were Emma Rose, and we want you now that you are Mattie Louise. Demon blood, ghost energy, and all. You are loved and you are wanted." A tear rolls down her cheek. "You are a Crane, and we don't care who you were or who'll you'll be. You are loved and you are wanted. Do you understand me, *ma petite chou*?"

I take a deep, steadying breath. Family. It's all I've ever wanted, and it's right here for the taking. They love me. They don't care if I'm part demon or not. They love me despite that.

You are loved and you are wanted.

I grew up feeling unloved and unwanted. I didn't even know what love was, not until Dan taught me. Here these people are offering me the most coveted thing a foster kid could ever hope for. Love and acceptance.

"Do you understand me, *ma petite chou*?"

I nod, unable to speak. I am wanted and loved, and it is the most precious thing in the world. I have a family who cares if I live or die. Strangers they might be, but I'm willing to give them a shot.

"Good." Lila's voice turns brisk again. "We brought you gifts. Ezekiel says you love to draw. We brought you a small mountain of sketch books, canvas, paints, pencils, anything we could think of. Your mother was an exceptional artist as well. I think your father still has some of her work at the plantation in New Orleans."

Her drawl is thick when she says New Orleans, only she pronounces it Naw'lins. I've seen people on TV get offended if you say it any other way.

"Yes, I do. It's all in the attic, if I remember correctly." Zeke moves over to the couch and sits. "Her work was very good, but it's nothing like Mattie's. Our girl's is hauntingly beautiful. The images stay with you days later. She's brilliant."

He grins at me like a proud papa. How can I not love him? He doesn't care about my upbringing. He just cares about me. Maybe after all this is over and done, I will go to New Orleans with him, if only to see where I come from.

I wander over and plop down beside him. It puts him between me and the grandparents since I'm next to the sofa arm. I might understand their feelings toward me, but I still need time to adjust. It's weird and unsettling and exciting all at once.

"Your father told us about your mother's name." Josiah takes a seat in the sofa chair to my right, allowing his wife to sit beside Zeke. "I did some digging into Georgina and found out quite a bit. You were right in that you have a brother."

"What?" Seriously?

My grandfather nods. "He's in college, Yale. His name is Alaric Dubois Buchard. His father, Richard Buchard, died when the boy was just a little thing. His grandparents raised him. Georgina was always a little...unstable. They feared she might hurt the boy."

"How do you know all this?"

"His grandfather and I are old friends. We went to Yale together. They live in Atlanta now, and I haven't laid eyes on him in over twenty years. He got quite a start when I called him up asking about his daughter. They haven't seen her in a long time. She remarried about a year after her husband's death, and they up and disappeared together. He always assumed the worst."

"Well, that could be why she refused to marry me," Zeke mused. "Perhaps because she was still married."

Plausible.

"Did you tell him about me?" Zeke said they dealt in bad juju, but if I have a brother, I want to meet him.

"No." Josiah shook his head. "I said we'd run across Georgina and it reminded me to call him up and shoot the breeze. I don't know what your father's told you about the Dubois family, Mattie, but they are not good people. They deal in things even we don't, and that's saying something. I'd like to have our investigator do some digging before I let them near you, especially given your talents."

"You think they might want to use me to gain more power?" Crazy people beget crazy people.

"Unfortunately, yes. We need to be able to protect you before they come within a thousand miles of you."

"She has the added protection of a Guardian Angel." Zeke yawns and his mother reaches over and slaps his knee. He gives her a "what" look. So like me. I want to laugh at his disgruntled expression.

"Manners." Lila glares at her son, and I can't help the giggle that escapes. I've never seen this before, this whole family interaction thing. It's quite entertaining.

"As I was saying, she has a Guardian Angel, and a Keeper of the Sword of Truth is tethered to her. I think she's safe from almost anything with those two watching over her."

Yeah, probably not the best time to mention my Guardian Angel is cursed and might be forced to kill me.

"Either way, we'll need contingency plans for her safety if we plan on introducing her." Lila stands. "Ezekiel told us about another potential problem as well. Deleriel."

The fallen angel who's currently soul sucking little kids. Yeah, big problem, and the most pressing one at the moment.

I can deal with homicidal family members tomorrow.

"We think he took the little girl who lives next door." I sit straighter. "Dan saw something earlier that makes him think Deleriel might be possessing a human or maybe using a human to nab the kids."

"He saw him?" Zeke looks alarmed. "Most who see a fallen angel don't live to tell about it."

"Maybe that's the wrong wording." I explain to them about Dan's new ability and everything he'd seen. "So maybe he's working with a human?"

"He wouldn't need to." Zeke rubs his chin thoughtfully. "He'd just appear and take them."

"Not if he's feeding." Josiah shakes his head. "The demon has a small army of fiends he's created using the fallen husks of the dead. He needs to feed them. Yes, Deleriel would do his own feeding, but when they all awake, they're ravenous. He'd need someone to torture the little ones until their souls are raw and bleeding to appease his children."

"Holy crap." My eyes widen, remembering that thing I'd seen in the morgue.

Lila bites her tongue at my language, but I don't even care.

"Zeke, I saw something this morning at the hospital morgue. I think I saw Deleriel and one of his creatures."

"Explain." The words are clipped, but it's because he's scared. I can see it in his expression.

I tell him all about my adventure in as much detail as I can.

"Aside from the yellow eyes, that sounds a lot like the ghost that was here last night. The one that attacked you. Do you remember it at all?"

The ghost from last night is a big old blank. I shake my head, trying my best to force the memory, but I get nada. "I wish I could, but no."

"It's not a wonder either," Lila fusses. "You went through some serious trauma yesterday. The mind can only take so much before it protects itself. You'll remember in time, but for now, don't fret about it."

Easier said than done. I hate not remembering things.

"I was thinking we could all go out to eat tonight." Zeke moves the conversation away from the ghostly visitors and back to more normal things. "There's a lovely Creole restaurant downtown you'll love, Mama. The gumbo is almost as good as back home."

"Dinner would be nice." She smooths her hair down. "Why don't we go at, say, seven? That gives Mattie a little while to rest up, and perhaps she can bring her young man down to meet us?"

"He's not my…he's…"

"Whatever he is, we'd love to meet him." Lila smiles, her eyes sparkling with laughter. "Ezekiel says we owe him your life several times over."

"Why don't you go check on him?" Zeke nods toward the open door. "He looked a little unsteady when he came in. I'm still worried about that head wound of his."

"Yeah, I can do that."

I stand and flee the room, still thinking of Lila calling him my young man.

Unexpected and unsettling after that soul wrenching kiss of his. I do need to check on him, though. Zeke's right about the head wound. Add in a nose bleed that wouldn't stop, and you get potentially disastrous problems.

I knock on the door and push it open, not waiting for a response. I find him sprawled out on the bed, passed out cold. He's been up and plowing through the day, but he needed to rest. I tried to tell him that all day. I guess his body finally made the decision for him.

Closing the door behind me, I head for my chair, and sure enough, my backpack from last night is still there. Inside are my sketchpad and favorite pencils. Drawing calms me, and after the day I've had, I need some Zen time. Taking my stuff out, I open the pad to a blank page and start to draw.

I think about this morning, and the morgue monsters begin to come to life on my page. I pour everything I'm feeling into it—fear, joy, pain, grief, everything. It's over an hour later when I finally stretch my fingers and look at my work.

It's so vivid, the images on the paper could be real. The details are exact, the impressions dark and forbidding. It's good, even by my standards.

"Much more impressive than your mother."

I nearly screech at the sound of Silas's voice. The demon is standing right behind me, staring intently at the page. His eyes are almost blue today. If I look at them just right, they do look blue and not black.

"What are you doing here, Silas? *How* are you here?"

Zeke has the place demon-proofed. He told me so.

Silas's grin is wicked, like that of a Cheshire cat. "I have my ways, Emma Rose."

He also refuses to call me anything but Emma Rose.

"If Zeke finds you here…"

He waves the threat off. "I came to check on you."

"Check on me?" Suspicion starts to build. I've never known Silas to care about anything but himself. "Why?"

"Can I not just care about your wellbeing, my darling girl?"

"No."

He laughs. "Well, I do. Care about your wellbeing, that is. I need you to accomplish my goals, and if you are dead, you cannot help me."

"Your goals?" He's alluded to needing me to do something for him before, but he never quite tells me what that is.

"None of your concern for now." He lays a hand up on my head, and a warm sensation floods me, causing me to shudder violently.

"What are you doing?" I hate the weird feeling running through me. It's unnerving.

"Healing you, so be quiet."

"I'm fine. If you want to heal someone, heal Dan."

"What will you give me if I do?"

"My thanks."

He chuckles, and it sets off alarm bells. It's a humorless laugh full of darkness. It reminds me he's a demon capable of unimaginable horrors. Silas scares the bejesus out of me.

"It doesn't work like that, my darling girl. The sooner you understand that, the sooner you can start making your own deals."

"I'm not making any deals, Silas, with you or anyone else."

"I know your father told you about your maternal lineage. You're a demon, Emma Rose. You need to start learning how to be a good little demon. Now that Deleriel is here and has his sights set on Mary, you really need to learn how to harness your demon side."

He picks up my hair and starts to braid it.

Mary? I remember Eli telling me something about this earlier, but with Dan and then Eric, I hadn't paid much attention. "What do you mean he has his sights set on Mary?"

"Didn't she tell you? Well, she may not have had time with everything going on. The child she went and cared for across the street was one of Deleriel's chosen. He only feeds upon souls that are a little broken, but still hold an edge of goodness and purity to them. That child had been passed from home to home, never really able to bond with a parent. His soul was broken. Mary stood up to Deleriel and his demonic children. He took a shine to the girl and has decided to take her with him when he goes back to his lair."

"He can't have her!"

"He's an upper level demon, Emma Rose. One of the first demons created when the angels fell from heaven. He's the right hand of the Morning Star. Who are we to stop him?"

"You're afraid of him!" Silas' fingers stop braiding and I can feel them flex in my hair. I'm right. He's afraid of Deleriel. If this thing scares Silas, then I'm doomed.

"Afraid is a strong word. Cautious would be a more accurate word. And he's also my employer."

"What?" He works for the super scary demon?

"Unfortunate, but true." He tisks at a wayward strand of hair. "He owns me."

Which explains why he's terrified of the guy.

"What Deleriel wants, Deleriel gets. I know this firsthand. I've lived it. Can you imagine what he'd do to a soul as pure as Mary's? The suffering it would go through? The torture he'd make her endure?"

That blind rage from earlier comes rushing back in, and a low growl starts in my chest, building until I'm up and shaking with rage. No one is touching Mary.

"Come here, my darling girl." Silas maneuvers me to stand in front of the mirror. "Tell me what you see."

"My eyes are black." Demonic eyes. It should terrify me, but I'm so focused on Mary and that monster wanting her, I don't care.

"Look closer, Emma Rose. Tell me what else you see."

I stare at myself for a long moment before a shocked gasp fills the room. My eyes aren't just black. I can see a sheen of yellow in them. The same yellow in that kid's eyes from my dream, the same yellow in the morgue kid's eyes. Why are my eyes yellow?

"Your mother's father wasn't the man who raised her." Silas yanks on my hair, pulling the braid tighter. "He was a demon who surfaced when he was summoned to help create a child who would hold immense power. Only she couldn't do what had been promised. She couldn't bring images to life."

Fudgepops.

"It required more than the Dubois had to offer. Delieriel was furious. He almost killed Georgina, but she was a smart one, your mother. She made a deal."

"A deal?" I don't like where this is going. Not one bit.

"She promised him a child who could do what he wanted, a child who could bring images to life with her blood. She was to give him the girl upon her second birthday. By then she'd know if the child was capable of doing the thing she could not."

"And he accepted the deal?"

Silas nods, a black scrunchie appearing in his hands. "She called me and wanted to know if I could help her get the recipe just right."

"And of course you could."

He smiled, the danger in his expression unmistakable. "I'd been making plans for two centuries, my darling girl. I set the wheels into motion a long time ago. The first piece of the puzzle came together in New Orleans with a woman named Elizabeth. Elizabeth came from a line of extremely gifted Shamans. She needed a child, and I was more than happy to provide that child. He later married and had a daughter, who married into the Crane family."

Holy crap. It can't be…

"You see, Emma Rose, you belong to me because I made you. I worked and cheated and stole and manipulated to make sure you were born with all the right gifts. The gifts Deleriel would pay a high price to own."

I can't breathe as the implication of his words echo in my ears. Would he trade me to Deleriel? Would he hand me over to the monster that scares him? If it meant his freedom? In a heartbeat.

"What do you want, Silas?"

"To protect you from him, of course."

He smooths down the stray strands of hair sticking out of the braid. "You're my granddaughter. It was I who convinced Georgina to let Claire whisk you away before Deleriel collected what he was due. You're alive because of me, Emma Rose. Your mother would have skinned you alive and fed your bones to Deleriel's demonic children had I not tricked her."

Zeke told me she'd been acting weird, standing over my crib. He said he'd been concerned about my safety. Maybe he had a right to do it.

"Why would she have done that? Couldn't she have just given me to him and been done with it?"

"Nothing is as simple as that." Silas inspects my braid. "A child cannot consent to giving up its soul. Only a parent can do that. Your mother agreed, but in order for Deleriel to obtain your gifts, you had to suffer, your soul bruised and bloody. Tortured. Your mother happily agreed to do that. She didn't love you, Mattie. She never did. To her, you were a means to an end. She made sure you were happy and felt loved because you had to be that bright bubbly soul for their plans to work. You feared your father's intentions, when it was your mother's you should have been concerned with."

"But Zeke said after I went missing, she fell into a depression."

"A punishment. Deleriel was furious she'd let you out of her sight. He imprisoned her in her mind where he delights in torturing her. If she ever wakes up and sees you, run, Emma Rose. Run fast and far. She'll kill you for all the suffering that's been inflicted upon her because of you."

If Silas advises running, I think I might need to heed the warning. "So how come no one could find me? Surely a demon as powerful as Deleriel could locate me?"

"Again, it was my foresight that prevented that. I'd placed a protection spell on you the day you were born. The moment your nanny took you, I activated it. It kept you hidden from everyone. Still does. Except for me. I can always find you because you are my flesh and blood,

Emma Rose."

"I still don't understand what you want from me, Silas."

"You're mine, Emma Rose, and I protect what's mine."

"Until it becomes more profitable for you not to do so." He's a demon. He makes deals every day, all day. It's who he is.

"Possibly." He tilts his head and leans down, laying his cheek against mine. "But for now, you are more valuable to me than anything or anyone else, and I'll protect you so long as you agree to help me."

"Help you?"

"To destroy Deleriel. It's what I bred you to do. You're the only one who can."

He wants me to fight a fallen angel? Not any fallen angel either. One of the first fallen angels, friend of Lucifer and all that. He's out of his freaking mind!

"Now, now, calm down." He flicks a glance at Dan. "We wouldn't want your friend there to suffer any more than he already is, now, would we?"

"You won't touch him."

"No, I won't. But my little pets will."

That's when I hear the growl, low and menacing. The bed bounces, and I can see the impression in the mattress. Something is sitting on the bed with Dan. Something big.

"Hellhound." Silas grins fondly in the direction of the bed. "Loyal beasts, but they do have a nasty habit of playing with their food."

"Get it away from him, Silas."

"You see, they like the smell of blood. First, she'd use her claws and rip him up a bit, digging across his chest, down his arms and legs. Enough to make him scream. Then she'd go for the juiciest parts…his stomach. She'd open it and eat all the gooey parts inside."

"I hate you." There's not a danged thing I can do either. She's sitting right there next to Dan.

"I know, my darling girl, I know." He turns me back toward the mirror. "I am sorry for what had to be done to wake up your demonic side. I had no idea the boy was injured when I left. I thought he'd just cuckolded himself." He lays his

277

cheek against mine and I can smell his breath. Peppermints. He smells like peppermints. Odd a demon should smell like a candy that reminds me of Christmas. "You and I, Mattie, are cut from the same cloth. We see what's directly in front of us and will hurt others to protect our own. We've both done it."

I want to argue with him, but I can't. By keeping Dan with me, I upset the balance, and people died. Innocent people. And I'd do it all over again. For Dan, I'd let them all die over and over if it meant keeping him safe. The sly grin tilting Silas's lips tells me he knows it too.

"Have you been practicing your gift?" He keeps his eyes on our image in the mirror.

"No."

A heavy sigh rolls through him. "Emma Rose, the only way to defeat him is through your gift. You have to be able to utilize it. If you can't do this, he gets Mary, and he keeps taking poor souls and feeding the rest to his hungry horde. You saw what happens to those little ones.

You met his very first child. In your dreams. You remember him, don't you?"

Yes, I remember him and the screams of that kid all those little creatures had descended upon.

"You are beginning to test my patience, child. I don't tell you to do something just to hear myself talk. Up until now, I've indulged you. You're my favorite, you know. I have other children, other grandchildren. None of them even comes close to your raw power. They don't have your strength, your courage. No matter how much I admire you, I will teach you a lesson. There are so many things I can do to torture you that won't kill you. I can even strip the flesh from your bones and put it all back together again."

His moves and his hand comes up to cup my cheek then clamps it over my mouth, trapping me with his body against the dresser. His other hand comes up, and the fingernail on his left hand digs into the soft skin of my cheek, tearing into it. A scream tries to escape as I watch him peel a strip of skin away from my face. It falls, hanging over the hand he has clamped against my mouth. He rubs the exposed tissue and muscle. Salt. His finger feels like salt on an open wound.

I heave, the queasiness surging up into my throat. The pain is unbearable.

"You see, Emma Rose? Even I have my limits. You will do as you are told, or you will be punished. Favorite or not, you are going to do as you're told."

He snaps his fingers and the wound is gone, the skin whole and unbroken, the pain gone as if it were never there, but the memory of it remains burned in my mind. He's crazy.

"You have one main task, Emma Rose. Learn to use your gift. When the time comes to face Deleriel, you must be ready. If you're not, you will find yourself in an unimaginable hell. One you will never escape. He will devour you, strip you of your gifts, and torture you for an eternity. Prepare yourself."

And he's gone. Just like that, he's gone as quickly as he'd appeared. A quick check of the bed proves his beast is gone as well. My fingers trace where the missing strip of flesh had been. It's unblemished, but I can still feel it there, feel the pain of watching his fingernail strip it down.

Silas is insane.

And my grandfather.

How messed up is that? Demonic bloodlines on both sides of the family. Should I tell Zeke? I mean, he should know about his demonic bloodlines. But part of me is shouting *no*. It's an instinct I've never ignored before, and I'm not about to start now. I'll deal with this on my own. Even if it means talking to someone I don't want to.

Dan's phone is lying on the nightstand beside the bed.

There is one person who might be able to help me. One person who lied repeatedly to me.

I pick up the phone and type in Dan's passcode. He uses the same one for everything. I scroll through his contacts until I see the name Lawrence Olivet. I sit back down in the chair and stare at the name. Then I look at Dan. He trusts Doc, and I trust Dan, so maybe I should trust

Doc at least enough to ask for help. If he tries anything, the entire Crane clan is here. He won't get away with it.

Decision made, I press the call icon and wait. He picks up on the third ring. "Dan?"

"No, it's Mattie."

"Mattie? Is everything okay? Why are you calling from Dan's phone?"

"Because I don't have my phone." I really need to figure out what happened to it.

"Oh." There's a pause, a long pause. "Mattie, about last night…"

"I don't want to talk about last night." I'm not ready to listen to his explanations. "I need to talk to you about something else."

"Of course. All I want to do is help."

"Have you ever heard of a fallen angel by the name of Deleriel?"

"Where did you hear that name?" His voice is deathly quiet, so quiet I almost don't hear it.

"I'm pretty sure that's who is kidnapping and murdering all the kids here in Charlotte. He's feeding."

"He feeds off the tortured souls of the innocent."

"Figured that part out already. He's apparently set his sights on Mary, and I need to know how to stop him, or at least keep him from getting his hands on my sister."

"I don't think you can, Mattie. He's one of the first demons, more powerful than anything I've ever come up against."

"Not what I need to hear right now, Doc. He can't have my sister."

"There's a solution here, Mattie. What, I don't know just yet. Let me do some research, okay? I need to talk to a few people, check some ancient texts. If there's a way to keep Mary safe, we'll find it. I promise."

The fact that he didn't say "destroy the demon" doesn't inspire a whole lot of confidence. Doc's always the first person to see the glass as half full. He's only seeing the water pouring out and circling the drain in this situation.

"Well, call Dan's phone if you find anything. Thanks." I hang up before he can try to start another conversation about me finding him at the Cross house last night with a picture of me and my mom.

Dan lets out a snore, and I gape at him. He'd slept through Silas, the Hellhound, and my conversation with Doc. He'd be proud of me for swallowing my pride and calling Doc. Not sure that atones for that snore he just let rip.

It has seriously been a day. I woke up to dealing with Meg's and Jake's deaths. I went from there to learning about my demonic heritage, then to dealing with a missing kid, to ghostly adventures in the morgue. My day then went down the drain starting with Eli's curse, discovering Dan has deeper feelings than he led me to believe, dealing with grandparents, and then Silas. Freaking Silas.

And the day still isn't over. I have to go to dinner with said family.

After that? Figure out where Kayla is before she dies, learn to use my gift of bringing images to life, and oh yeah, destroying a demon that's pretty much bulletproof.

Just another day in the life of Mattie Louise Hathaway.

The End of Book 4 Part 1

Acknowledgements

Every time I finish a book, it hits me how blessed I am. My grandma always said God gave each of us a talent. Sometimes we don't know what that talent is and sometimes we ignore it or squander it away. I ignored mine for a long time because I was afraid. You go and write this bright shiny new book, but then freeze up. Sharing something you created with everyone is scary. Terrifying really. It was my Gran who finally gave me the courage to try. She told me God blessed me not only with a big imagination, but with the gift of words to go along with it. Told me I needed to use it. And I'm so grateful I did because of how truly blessed it's made me.

I gained an army of readers who love my silly nonsense words, who love my characters, and enable me to finally do a job I love: writing. If you love what you do, it's never work. I'm lucky enough to be able to write full time and that is because of that army of readers so thank you to all the fans and all the readers who enable me to do what I love.

Writing is hard, getting published is even harder. I did something everyone told me NOT to do, I trusted a small publisher—Limitless Publishing. It was the best decision I ever made. Am I in big box brick and mortar stores or major bookstore shelves? No, but I hope they will eventually hire someone to do just that. They gave me something no one else did. They believed in my work when everyone else, the agents and the big publishers said nope, not today chickie. You're just not good enough, but Limitless believed I was. They took a chance on me when no one else would. And that matters to me. It's why I'm still with Limitless Publishing. The people who work there are fabulous. They take care of me, put up with my madness, and deal with my quirks. Jennifer, Jessica, Dixie, and Elise, I can't put into words how grateful I am to all of you for all you do. Thank you for being the kind of people who care about their authors. We're not just numbers to you, but people. That means a lot.

My editor…Lori Whitwam. You have taught me so much and made me a better writer. I've learned to focus my thoughts more on paper and that less really is more in a lot of instances. You push me, challenge me, and always work with me even when I drive you nuts with my crazy timelines. Thank you for being an awesome editor and an even better friend. You're the best.

My family puts up with a lot when I'm writing. They keep me fed and remind me to shower. They don't mind the pajama bottoms and ratty t-shirts I have on when I write. Thank you guys for just being there and encouraging me. Especially my dad. He always believes in me and gets just as excited as I do when I finish a book. He bites his nails on release day same as I do. My Daddy is awesome. ☺

This book required a lot of police work, especially dealing with the first few hours of a missing child. A big thank you to all the officers who contacted me over Facebook and Twitter. You guys helped so much in the writing of the protocols here. Thank you, thank you, thank you!!

And last, but not least, a huge thank you to all The Ghost Files fans. You guys are why I continue to write this series. All your emails and messages and comments on my Facebook page and Wattpad page are so very appreciated. They keep me going. I love all of my readers so much. My Ghost Files fans are hardcore and I adore that about y'all. Thank you from the bottom of my heart.

About the Author

So who am I? Well, I'm the crazy girl with an imagination that never shuts up. I LOVE scary movies. My friends laugh at me when I scare myself watching them and tell me to stop watching them, but who doesn't love to get scared? I grew up in a small town nestled in the southern mountains of West Virginia where I spent days roaming around in the woods, climbing trees, and causing general mayhem. Nights I would stay up reading Nancy Drew by flashlight under the covers until my parents yelled at me to go to sleep.

Growing up in a small town, I learned a lot of values and morals, I also learned parents have spies everywhere and there's always someone to tell your mama you were seen kissing a particular boy on a particular day just a little too long. So when you get grounded, what is there left to do? Read! My Aunt Jo gave me my first real romance novel. It was a romance titled "Lord Margrave's Deception." I remember it fondly. But I also learned I had a deep and abiding love of mysteries and anything paranormal. As I grew up, I started to write just that and would entertain my friends with stories featuring them as main characters.

Now, I live in Huntersville, NC where I entertain my niece and nephew and watch the cats get teased by the birds and laugh myself silly when they swoop down and then dive back up just out of reach. The cats start yelling something fierce...lol.

I love books, I love writing books, and I love entertaining people with my silly stories.

Facebook:

https://www.facebook.com/authorAprylBaker

Twitter:

https://twitter.com/AprylBaker

Wattpad:

http://www.wattpad.com/user/AprylBaker7

Website:

http://www.aprylbaker.com/

Newsletter:

http://www.subscribepage.com/n0d6y8

Printed in Great Britain
by Amazon